Quenchless Fire

(The second Matthias Barton medieval mystery)

by
Rosie Lear

**Grosvenor House
Publishing Limited**

This book is published by
Grosvenor House Publishing Ltd
Link House
140 The Broadway, Tolworth, Surrey, KT6 7HT.
www.grosvenorhousepublishing.co.uk

This book is a work of fiction but based upon real-life historical events
and characters. The story is a product of the author's imagination and
should not be construed as true.

A CIP record for this book
is available from the British Library

ISBN 978-1-78623-357-8

For my children
Now flown
Richard, Edward
Rachel, Sophie

Then you compared a woman's love to hell
To barren land, where water will not dwell,
And you compared it to a quenchless fire,
The more it burns the more is its desire
To burn up everything that burnt can be.

Chaucer..Canterbury Tales.

Chapter 1

The dusty trackway stretched in front of the man, leading downwards towards Purse Caundle. The heat of the day, coupled with a troublesome breeze, blew dust and grit from the track into his one good eye; the other had been blinded in battle. Sweat trickled uncomfortably from his hairline and down his haggard face, but he was unable to wipe it away lest he lose his balance; he needed both hands on his make-shift crutches. His body was bent over them - he had not been able to find sticks the same length when the crutches given by the good nuns had been stolen from him as he slept. He gritted his discoloured teeth and stared hungrily at the track ahead. It shimmered dangerously in the heat and he bit on his dry lips, trying to swallow away the cruel dryness in his mouth.

His steps were becoming slower and slower as he dragged himself onwards. It was a mission of pilgrimage as well as loyalty, but he wished fervently that he had not undertaken it. His destination was close but his endurance was nearing its end.

He had travelled only from Sherborne that day; he had been put ashore at Melcombe a week ago and had worked his way painfully towards his first destination. This was his fourth day on the journey. With matted hair, mud-caked clothes and dirty bitten hands, no carter would stop and offer a lift to such a man, his amputated stump giving him a decidedly awkward, even frightening gait.

He paused to lean on a fallen tree. With his sticks resting against the tree stump, he wiped the sticky sweat from his unshaven face. He had found a piece of discarded twine with which to bind the hair from his face, but this had become loose and he dragged his hair away from his hot face in frustration. His weariness and despair returned as he rested. Being discharged wounded had seemed a good idea, but once he was put ashore with other such men, he was alone.

Despite his appearance he was a man of honour. He had tried every possible argument with Allard, reasoning with him long into the night, but Allard's mind was made up, and since it was Allard who had carried him out of battle and had helped to hold him during that terrifying amputation, this was his only way of repaying what he considered to be a debt....even a pilgrimage of sorts. He had prayed to die, indeed his frantic, sobbed prayers had almost been answered in those black and desperate afterdays. Many had died, but he had not. However, he was now no use to any battle unit and he had made his way to port and so to England. He was penniless, frightened, hungry, in constant pain, but determined to return home.

His home was a small village near Shaftesbury but first he needed to visit Allard's wife. Whatever had befallen him, he was still an honourable man, a man who felt his honour keenly. What Allard had chosen to do was not right...was not chivalrous or honest, but it was his decision, and it was right that his Lady should know. He grasped his sticks and propelled himself upright, taking a moment or two to regain his balance enough to take a few steps.

There were dwellings now in his restricted sight. He stumbled forward, eager to have this ordeal over. The mellow stone of the village seemed welcoming...his ears heard the soft lowing of cattle...a song from a nearby barn...children playing in a brook watched his approach in silence and ran indoors crying out in fear.

He pushed himself on. Allard had once described the house to him in detail...there it was now in front of him...a gate-house...leading into a stable-yard...as he stumbled into the yard a servant opened a door leading to an outhouse. She gasped in horror and ran back into the scullery from whence the cook emerged...a large red-faced woman, capped and aproned, arms akimbo.

"Be off, or I'll fetch our steward."

The man leaned exhausted on a stone water butt.

"I've come to speak with the Lady Alice."

"The Lady Alice does not live here – but she'll not see you, I warrant. How dare you come here with such demands."

Another door opened further in and an older man emerged. His being clearly portrayed him as the steward of the household; his large hands looked capable, his shoulders were strong, his apparel clean and neat. He wore a thick belt over his russet brown doublet with a jangle of keys attached. His tunic of dyed wool under the doublet reached to his knees, and his dark hose ended in soft shoes suitable for house wear. Deep set eyes under bushy eyebrows looked the man up and down in silence.

"Please," breath and speech were slow in coming after his tortuous journey, "I bear news from Sir Allard."

Thomas the steward, like his master, had seen action in battle and recognised the situation rather better than the cook.

"Wait here. I will fetch Sir Tobias."

He disappeared into the house and the man waited, leaning painfully against the butt, his strength and resolve dissolving into utter weariness and despair.

Sir Tobias was the King's Coroner in Dorset, a man much admired amongst his peers for his honesty, integrity and expertise. He too had seen battle in France and recognized immediately the total exhaustion of the man leaning in his yard.

He led him through the kitchen into a small comfortably furnished parlour and gestured him to a wooden settle.

"My name is Martin Cooper." His ragged breathing made his words jerky, "I have been acting as squire to Sir Allard for the past two years." He paused, his mouth dry, his heart pounding painfully. His stump throbbed unbearably. Sometimes he wished Allard had left him to die. What could life hold for him now? He felt dirty, the lowest of the low before this upright lord. He gazed at Sir Tobias with his one good eye, and saw a face filled with understanding rather than pity. Understanding he could manage, but pity was despicable.

"You have news of my son-in-law?"

Martin swallowed. This man had seen fighting and had acquitted himself with honour. What would he do when he heard what Martin had to tell him?

A serving girl brought ale, and Martin drank greedily, glad to slake his thirst and postpone the giving of news for a few seconds more.

"The message is for Lady Alice," he faltered.

"My daughter is under my protection whilst Sir Allard is fighting in France. I will give her the message,"

Martin dropped his head in his hands. Images of Allard passed through his mind. He had tried so hard to prevent Allard from his course of action, but he would not be dissuaded. At least he, Martin, had played no part in it. Allard had finally acted alone, although Martin held most of the details in his heart.

"Sir Allard has deserted his post." The sentence hung in the room like a cold stone. There – he had uttered it.

Sir Tobias felt the chill of the words and the desperation of his daughter in one combined blow. The silence in the room deepened; only Martin's ragged breathing broke the silence.

"How could his happen? Allard was surely a good captain?"

Martin remembered the early days, when Allard was indeed a good model for his men. In the two years he had acted as squire to the young knight, they had seen battle together many times. Allard had not shirked from his duties as leader of his men, and had been included in talks with generals of strategies. He had insisted his men keep their target practice in good shape and knew how to inspire them with courage.

Then had arrived Celeste, a camp follower of French origin, golden haired, voluptuously proportioned, daringly funny – yes – very good company for all the men, but particularly for Allard. Their captain had been much taken with the lively, funny, intelligent girl, a very different kind of courtesan. The attachment had grown disastrously strong. Allard would do nothing without Celeste.....they were more together in soul than anything Martin had experienced. Allard had spoken of his resentment at his marriage, how he had never experienced such joy in a woman as he had with Celeste, how pale and insignificant Alice was in comparison. This much he knew he could never tell Sir Tobias, much less Alice. These things must be kept in his heart.

"Sir Allard asked me to tell Lady Alice that he will not be returning, that he is sorry for any hurt caused, and that she is to consider him as one dead."

"But he is not dead, and his marriage vows exist."

Hot shame burned through Sir Tobias. This was dishonourable, shameful – and deeply wounding for Alice and Luke, her little son. Shame and anger joined together as Sir Tobias berated Martin for the news he had brought. Why had Martin not discouraged the liaison – as Sir Allard's squire he could have done so – he had watched this develop, why had he not tried to banish the girl from the camp…why had Martin not sought help from their liege lord before Allard's final decision.

Eventually the anger was spent. Martin sat with tears rolling down his face as the arrows of accusation poured down on him. His own desperation and exhaustion were complete and utterly overwhelmed him.

"Why did Allard send you?" demanded Sir Tobias, roughly. He was not a rough man and hated the sound of his own voice as he spoke, but his anger and shame for Alice was great and was making him unreasonable.

Perhaps this was the worst part, Martin thought.

"Sir Allard did not send me, my lord. I came voluntarily, without Allard's knowledge."

"But you gave me to believe that you had a message from my son-in-law."

"I did. That is what Allard told me he would say if he could find a messenger. After that I was sorely wounded, as you can see. Allard carried me to safety and insisted on surgeon's knives rather than a diseased death. When I was sufficiently recovered he had gone."

Understanding of the man's motives flooded over Sir Tobias. He stood and touched Martin gently on the shoulder.

"You have more than fulfilled the duties of a squire. I thank you."

Martin wiped his eyes on his torn sleeve.

"Give me more details. I must prepare what I am to say to my daughter."

Martin's tired mind sifted the details carefully. Some he must leave out. Allard had become aware of the woman, Celeste, some eighteen months gone. As their friendship had blossomed into love, Allard had become less caring for his men. He had even exhibited a degree of cruelty towards one or two of the younger men which Martin had not seen before, and which he did not like. However, Allard had confided in him just after Christmas Mass that he could not bear to leave Celeste, that his days of loyalty to the Duke and therefore the young King were over, and he would follow Celeste wherever they would go. Martin tried to reason with him...this was just a passing phase, he said, caused by his long absence from his true lady. Allard had bitten his head off – he had no true lady now but Celeste and wished he could find a messenger to carry such news to his wife so that her concern for him would cease.

During their time in Calais, the Duke of Bedford, who had led the men with such forceful strategies had died, and William de la Pole, the Duke of Suffolk, had returned to military service together with the young Richard, Duke of York, who led campaigns with Suffolk in the late Summer and early Autumn of 1436. The English had relinquished Paris and were now defending Normandy, still retaining their hold on Calais. Duke Humphrey, Duke of Gloucester, was still much concerned with advising the young King Henry in London, although after his brother Bedford's death he did attempt forays in Calais, without much success. Martin glossed over these, for he was aware that Sir Tobias would have known these commanders, and understood the increasing difficulty of campaigns. The reluctance of the son of Henry Vth, still only fourteen years old, to step into his father's shoes was becoming apparent, and the loss of the support of the Duke of Burgundy had turned the tide of the war against the English. Martin caught the brunt of the fighting but Allard had insisted on carrying him to the camp surgeon; by the time Martin was fully conscious and had become aware of his own perilous situation – now an amputee and blind in one eye – Allard had gone. His horse and all his belongings had been taken, and there appeared to be no-one who had seen him go – just gone, like a thief in the night. Celeste was seen no more.

Injured men were no use in this war and deserters were not sought actively…the battles continued without them. Allard's men drifted away, some to other lord's service, and some too wounded, like himself, had tried to make for England. Duke Humphrey, better placed to be in England, was replaced by the young Duke of York, but the change had come too late for Martin. They were without pay, had been thus for some time, and without horse or belongings, just thankful to be alive and on home soil – or not, Martin thought bitterly. Provisions in and out of Calais were intermittent and morale was low.

"Where are you making for now?" Sir Tobias asked him quietly. His anger was spent, indeed he knew his anger had been wrongly directed. It was no fault of Martin's.

"My mother has a dwelling in a small village near Shaftesbury. I must return there."

"My household will offer you rest before you travel on – it is the least I can do."

The kind offer brought easy tears to Martin's eyes again. The steward Thomas was instructed to show him to a small room and brought water for him with which to wash, a platter of bread, cheese and cold meat, and more watered ale. Soon a straw filled mattress appeared, and Thomas helped Martin discard his filthy clothes, bringing an old tunic to cover his shamed nakedness. Left alone, Martin sank down on the makeshift bed and fell deeply asleep.

Chapter 2

Sir Tobias bit the sides of his forefinger in agitation as he walked the length of his rose garden. His agile mind played over the information he had received. How could Allard have shamed himself so? What he had done amounted to treason, and there was no coming back from that. He would ride to Shaftesbury to speak with Allard's father....perhaps it was a fortunate thing that his mother had died some years previously.

As Coroner for the County of Dorset, Sir Tobias was himself a well respected and honest citizen. He could not hide this disgrace – it would be a dishonest thing to pretend Allard had died in battle, for that would make him a hero.

Sir Tobias had been in battle himself with Old King Henry; he knew battle; he knew the sounds, the smells, the clamour of the field. He understood the revulsion at the sights after the battle – the stench of blood...the terrified screams from injured horses kicking wildly in their death throes....the bubbling wounds of the dying. He had heard the imploring gasps from the injured, some begging for release, some trying to give last messages, some screaming obscenities at the very sky.....and after battle, for those remaining? Wood fire smoke scenting the air....meat cooking......a quiet thankfulness ...a shaken inner feeling that you were one of the lucky ones.

Sometimes wounded men would be brought into the camp surgeons by friends who had refused to let them die. Martin would have been one such man – and what would happen to Allard now? He had slipped camp with his horse, his leman and his belongings and gone where? To a far place, no doubt, where he could set up a life far distant from his wife and young son, living a life of eternal deception and dishonour. Men did this, he knew, - not many, - but some. He would never have thought it of Allard – he had truly believed he had secured his only daughter a good match, a solid union.

His lady wife was watching him, face concerned at his unusual pacing.

He took her hand gently and held it tightly in his own for a moment before leading her to the wall, warm in the sun to their touch. They sat together, husband and wife, she just a sentence away from her only daughter's heartbreak.

Sir Tobias told Martin's story haltingly, trying to soften the tale as he went, but there was no softening to be had. The truth of the matter, - the uncomfortable, distressing truth - was that their son-in-law Allard, a young knight of promise, a captain of men in the siege of Calais fighting against the men of Philip the Good under the command of Edmund Beaufort, had deserted his post – a treasonable offence – and disappeared with his leman, deserting also his young wife Alice and their son, Luke. He had left even as Duke Humphrey had arrived with ten thousand men for their relief, and had simply slipped away.

They sat together in silence, absorbing their son-in-law's disgrace and anticipating their beloved daughter's distress. They heard Luke's voice approaching the stable yard.

"William will take Luke riding." Lady Bridget rose and steadied herself on her husband's shoulder as he sat.

"I will organize it immediately. Will you talk to Alice now?"

Alone for a moment in the garden, Sir Tobias gave thanks for the practical common sense of his wife, as she left to organize a ride for the child Luke with Sir Tobias' squire, William.

Alice's frozen white face would stay with Sir Tobias for a long time. She sat as if carved in stone, still as a statue, marble-chilled. Her lips were stiff, her eyes closed as if she could not bear anyone to see the hurt and despair she felt. Much of the story as he had understood it from the man Martin, he omitted. There was hurt enough here without adding detail.

"He has left his post. He has deserted. He cannot come back. He may be caught and tried." Alice repeated the information in short clipped sentences. She raised her head and tried to breathe. She felt suffocated....she was drowning.... but she willed herself to behave with spirit and dignity.

"Then I must make my own way in life from now on. Father, I know this cannot be hidden dishonestly, but allow us to be discreet with this information."

"We will keep it, Alice, until we have learned to accept this ourselves."

"I will never learn to accept it," Alice said coldly, "And I would speak with the man before you allow him to go on his way."

"Do you think that is wise?"

"I care not whether it is wise or no, but I must hear this news personally from him."

"He is in poor condition, Alice. He has been blinded in one eye and has lost the lower part of one leg. He has been starved, spat upon for his deformities, abused by passers by, yet he came to offer you this knowledge. Do not be harsh with him."

She saw Martin the next day. He was clean, which served to emphasize his pallor. His blinded eye had been covered with a makeshift patch, and he was wearing an old tunic and hose found by William, Sir Tobias' squire, and someone had cut new crutches for him of a better size. He was weak, amazed by the kindness shown to him by this household to whom he had brought such unwelcome news. They had fed him, and he had been offered watered ale and a place to sleep. He was dreading the encounter with Alice - and then when it was over he would need to take his leave and continue with his own journey.

Alice had dressed carefully for this meeting. Her dark green gown trimmed with gold embroidered flowers around the hem and bodice was loosely belted with a fine gold chain. Her soft shoes made little sound on the tiled floor. She had braided her hair tightly under her wimple which framed a pale face with dark shadows under her eyes, the colour of her gown emphasising her strained complexion, but she carried herself proudly as she stepped into her father's small library of precious books.

The man was waiting for her, standing, balancing his weight carefully on his good side, with the help of his newly made sticks.

"You have news of my husband?"

Martin nodded.

"Then tell me the news,"

"I Thought Sir Tobias had…"

"I want to hear it myself from you," Alice snapped.

Martin breathed deeply. He did so hope she was not going to make this difficult.

Although he had been Sir Allard's squire for two years, he was not titled, wealthy or clever; he could never have aspired to be anything greater. He was simply an honest, kind, hardworking young man who had been fortunate in war to have appealed to Sir Allard and used as his squire when his original young squire had been taken by a fatal arrow wound to his neck, killing him instantly. Sir Allard had taught him all he needed to know about arming him for battle, caring for his expensive armour and any protocol that was necessary for a squire to adhere to. They had been of similar age and enjoyed the same sense of fun – until Celeste, that is. There was nothing for it – he would have to be direct.

"Sir Allard has deserted his post."

"Is that all you can tell me?"

"There's little else to tell, my Lady."

"Did you help him go?"

"No, my Lady, I was confined by the surgeon's knife – when I had recovered sufficiently to return to camp, he had left."

"Why have you come here? Did you expect money?"

Martin flushed at her stinging tone.

"I was his squire – I knew he had family who would wish to know of his wherabouts, my Lady,"

"Did he send you?"

"No, my Lady. He carried me from the battle when I was sorely wounded. He did not allow me to die in a ditch. This is payment of my debt to him for that."

Alice was silent. Martin lowered his eyes respectfully. There was a short silence before Alice asked, "With whom did he leave?"

The question fell in the room like a pebble in a dark, silent forest pool. Martin felt the chill. He was evasive.

"I was not there, my lady. I do not know."

"I don't believe you. You were his squire. You know full well what I mean."

Her voice was steely, her eyes were cold and hard. It was the only way she knew how to keep her composure.

"My Lady…"

"Don't 'My lady' me, soldier. Tell me what I need to know."

Martin swallowed hard. "He left with a lady."

"Her name?"

"Celeste."

"French?"

"Yes."

"Thank you for your honesty. I know now what I am."

She turned on her heel and left the room, her skirts swishing as she rounded the corner and disappeared from view.

Martin lowered himself cautiously onto the wooden bench, shaking with emotion. His task was done. He could now prepare to struggle on to Shaftesbury.

However, Martin was still at the Coroner's house two days later. Lady Bridget had organized a makeshift bed for him in the small room into which he had been taken at first. Both she and her husband were aware of the effort it had cost Martin to make the journey and were grateful to him, however unwelcome the news, and at their suggestion he had agreed to rest there until Sir Tobias could arrange a passing cart to take him further on his way. Once he had seen Martin safely on his way with a carter bound for Shaftesbury, Sir Tobias followed the next day to see Sir Alwyn, Allard's father.

Sir Alwyn received Sir Tobias cordially at first, but his demeanour changed as he listened to the story.

"The foolish pup!" he exploded. "How dare he disgrace our name!"

After some discussion he agreed that Alice should continue to live under her Father's protection and that a large portion of her marriage dowry should be returned to the family.

"But I want to be troubled no more by this," he said, after the wine goblets were emptied. "My son has not returned from France. That is all I am able to say, and should he ever try to return with his tail between his legs, I cannot give him a home. He is as one dead."

Sir Tobias noted that he did not dwell on Alice's distress nor did he ask after his grandson, Luke. He had carefully avoided the word 'treason,' too.

"I thought I was a good judge of men," he said to his wife on his return,

"It seems I was mistaken. I thought Allard to be a sound match for Alice, and I judged Sir Alwyn to be an upright man."

"He will erase Allard from his life then?"

"I fear so. I hope in time Alice will be able to do so, although for a different reason, but at present she is too shocked to do such a thing."

Alice seemed incapable of caring adequately for Luke over the next few weeks. Her initial steely composure crumbled and she was a broken reed. Luke looked tired and grubby, and Alice's maid servant took over his daily care. Alice busied herself with inconsequential matters and rode out several times with no purpose in mind except to leave the house and be alone. When she came to the house of Sir Tobias she refused to speak of Allard, or to enter into any discussion as to how she should move forward. Conversation was stilted. The old happy, carefree Alice of yesterday was gone. Her speech was clipped. She lost colour and spirit.

Sir Tobias rode over one day to see his young friend Matthias Barton at Milborne Port. Matthias had started a small school for boys in his own home. He hadn't seen Matthias for some months and he was pleased to see Matthias at work with his young pupils.

"I have a small favour to ask you, Matthias," he told him, as they relaxed on a grassy seat in the shade of a sweet chestnut tree. The Summer was becoming fully blown now, hot and sultry, and both men were glad of the shade.

"Alice has learned that her husband will not be home just yet. She has taken this very hard. Luke is neglected. I know he is too young for your school, but it would be a kindness if you would take him until Alice has recovered her spirits."

Matthias was taken aback, as well as being a little flattered. Whenever he had seen the Lady Alice she was more than mistress of any situation, and he had admired her from a distance, being unusually shy and uneasy in her presence. She laughed a great deal, and sometimes Matthias had suspected that she was laughing at his reticence. He knew Sir Tobias had hoped to educate Luke at the school in Sherborne, run by his friend Thomas Copeland for the monks at the Abbey.

"He is very young – only four years old."

"Nearly five, but much neglected at present, and somewhat confused by the change in his mother."

Matthias considered. He had five pupils at present, ranging in age from seven to ten years. They were all the sons of merchants rising in the world, who understood the value of education for their sons. Luke would be a baby amongst them.

"I am willing to try," he replied, scratching his head as he wondered how to tailor his lessons to one so young.

"William will bring him over tomorrow," Sir Tobias decided. "You could ride back with him in the afternoon and dine with us. We can then decide whether it is a plan that is workable."

Luke arrived the next morning on his fat little pony, chaperoned by William. Before leaving, William murmured to Matthias that the whole household was in a state of upheaval and tension to indicate that Luke's demeanour might be at odds with his normal self, and that Matthias might notice a difference when he brought him home at the end of the day.

With no further information forthcoming, Matthias assumed that Allard was either injured or taken prisoner, and set about making Luke comfortable in the schoolroom. He was impressed by the interest Luke showed in all that was going on, and Matthias quickly realised that Luke could read a little – Alice had not been lazy in teaching him what she herself had learned from her father.

However, when Matthias returned with Luke in the late afternoon, he was shocked and puzzled by the obvious tension in the family. Alice did not appear.

William stabled Luke's little pony in Sir Tobias' stables, and a maid servant took Luke away to wash and feed him elsewhere, although Matthias noticed that his anxious eyes were searching eagerly for his mother.

"Is the Lady Alice well?" Matthias asked, hesitantly, when the meal was finished.

"Wearied by the failure of Allard to return," Sir Tobias told him, finding it hard to put the truth into words.

"Was he expected home just now?" Matthias asked, puzzled, for there had never been any uneasiness surrounding Allard before. Matthias had always accepted that he was fighting in France and would return home in the fullness of time.

Sir Tobias paused. He exchanged a glance with the Lady Bridget. An imperceptible nod passed between them.

Matthias and Sir Tobias had forged an unlikely warm friendship when investigating the death of Ben, a young friend of Matthias' manservant, the previous Spring.

They had seen death together too much and too recently for Sir Tobias to fabricate to Matthias.

"We have been an unhappy household for the last three weeks, Matthias. A young squire, badly injured, called on us to bring unwelcome news from France.

Matthias caught his breath, - Allard was dead?

"Allard has deserted his post. He will not be returning home."

Matthias was stunned. He sensed the humiliation the family must feel, and the desperate hurt to Alice and Luke.

"I cannot keep this information secret, Matthias, but I have decided to tell only such people as can possibly begin to see how much damage this has done to Alice and Luke. I will not lie if challenged, but neither will I announce the news in the market place. We cannot allow people to assume he is dead, injured or taken prisoner, but we can say as little as possible without being deceitful."

"Thank you for your confidence in me," Matthias said, soberly.

"Alice has taken this very hard. She is frightened to contemplate her future and grieving for the husband she thought she had."

Matthias was thoughtful as he rode home in the gathering dusk. He could understand how very difficult the situation was for Sir Tobias, and how painful for Alice. He would be sure to keep a close eye on Luke in the coming weeks.

Chapter 3

The Summer droned on, hot and dry. Sherborne was a quarrelsome place to be in, not helped by the heat. Matters with Abbot Bradford were still not resolved. The Abbot of Sherborne was a haughty man, proud and unbending. He had recently caused the doorway between the Chapel of Ease, All Hallows, to be narrowed, making it more difficult for the ordinary townspeople to use it for processionals. All Hallows was joined to the Abbey, and had its own appointed priest in charge, currently one Richard Vowell. The good people of Sherborne had become very divided in this matter. Some had erected a new font in All Hallows to avoid having to use the narrowed entrance to the Abbey when Baptisms took place, and Abbot Bradford was incensed by this action. He demanded that the font should be demolished, for the baptising of children was his right, being performed in the main body of the Abbey, in the Abbey font. He had appealed to Bishop Neville of Salisbury, who had ordered that the doorway should be widened as it had been before, but also that the illegal font in All Hallows should be removed. But despite Bishop Neville's intervention, no effort had been made to widen the doorway or to remove the illegal font, and the townspeople continued to annoy the monks and the Abbot with their fire smoke and early morning bells. Some of the townspeople were on the side of the Abbot, but more of them were playing at being the indignant faction at war with the Abbey.

The narrow streets were hot, dirty and dusty. Women sat outside their humble dwellings on upturned barrels, skirts pulled up to their knees, thighs apart to try and capture some cool. Men sat around ale houses grumbling and quenching their thirst when they could afford it, wiping their sweaty foreheads with the backs of their dirty hands, leaving streaky sweat marks across their faces.

They resented the influence of the Abbey and the intransigence of Abbot Bradford. Mostly they craved simply a return to their straightforward rites of worship in All Hallows, Chapel of Ease. They deeply resented the supercilious Abbot and his prior and openly mocked the monks whenever they saw them.

Matters were hardly helped by the feeling that law and order was becoming fragile in the land; the previous Winter had been most bitterly cold, and now, with an extremely hot Summer, the crops looked in danger of failing. This would bring great hardship in the coming Winter. Men returning from France, disillusioned and bitter, just added to the boiling pot of increasing unease. His Grace King Henry had only just assumed his adult kingship, despite his tender years, and there was unrest among the nobles who were jostling for position, all greedy for their chance of preferment. Normally such affairs of state would not permeate to the peaceful towns so far away from the great capital. However, at present the air seemed filled with discontent and bile.

Matthias became aware of the unrest through Thomas Copeland, the appointed schoolmaster of the Sherborne Abbey School for boys, whom he called on whenever he had occasion to ride into Sherborne. Matthias had once been a pupil there himself, and had developed a warm respect for Master Thomas, who had mentored him in his own new school venture.

"It is becoming very uncomfortable, Matthias," Thomas told him, "Several of the townspeople have formed a group of protesters. They take it in turns to agitate against the Abbey. It will end in trouble."

Matthias observed such trouble himself. The monks were accustomed to putting waste food out from the guesten house door each day for the poor. Of late, the food had become less and was often rancid or stale. The monks were careless in the handling of it, and were apt to open their door, throw the food carelessly into the baskets and retreat without so much as a kind word or even effort at eye contact. Matthias heard raucous jeering as the door opened, and as the food was tossed towards the basket, several men stepped forward threateningly and threw well aimed clods of earth at the two monks, who retired hastily, but not before being spattered with mud by the missiles.

The protestors had agreed to harass the monks on a daily basis for their miserly offerings to the poor, so there were three or four small merchants and tradesmen present. A small crowd had gathered and there was angry rumbling from them. The beggars melted away, clutching what little food they had managed to grasp, unwilling to be the centre of attraction.

Sir Tobias experienced more of the unrest some little time later. An uneasy air of resignation had settled over the fine house at Purse Caundle. Luke continued to attend school with Matthias; Alice remained for the most part, aloof from daily affairs, whilst Lady Bridget presided with magnificent calm over the fractured household.

Alice would not discuss future arrangements for her life, aware in her own estimation that she was now no more than spoiled goods, and that she should agree to remain under the protection of Sir Tobias, in his household. In his wisdom, he did not press her, knowing her to be safe in the lodge house nearby with her own small household, but soon he would need to insist that she came to live within the family home, where she could be safe and provided for.

He had business in Sherborne and he, William and his scribe had occasion to use the George Hostelry at the top of Cheap Street to conclude some matters requiring his attention. As this was just a one day visit, he had brought Lady Alice with him to divert her. William chaperoned her to the market while Sir Tobias and the scribe completed their business and at the conclusion, they became aware that an unsavoury brawl had broken out at the bottom of Cheap Street, spilling into the Shambles and onto the Abbey Green.

Sir Tobias strode down the hill and halted half way down in dismay as he saw townspeople out in full array, some with staves, laying about their opponents, some fighting hand to hand, wrestling angrily with each other. William and Lady Alice were struggling through the crowd towards him. Market stalls had been overturned, women striving to recover spoilt goods. He saw milk running down into the leat at the bottom of the hill and dogs fighting over a stolen chicken from a butcher in the Shambles. A stout fellow lurched towards him, blood running down his face. He was wielding a pole and his tunic hung off him at a drunken angle.

Sir Tobias hustled his daughter into the shelter of the hostelry as he heard galloping horses from the distant castle. The bailiff had clearly sent for reinforcements.

Abbot Bradford emerged from his house near the Abbey and drew level with Sir Tobias.

"The Bishop must reinforce my authority," he said breathlessly. "There is dissension here the like of which I've never experienced – and the people are now fighting each other, friend against friend, neighbour against neighbour."

Sir Tobias was very well aware of Abbot Bradford's authoritarian manner – he had experienced it before during his investigation into the death of Ben Glover and others.

"Less antagonism all round would go a long way to resolving this unchristian dispute," he declared.

The two men watched silently as mounted soldiers from the castle rode hard through the crowd, dividing them and kicking them here and there to disarm these angry men, who were forced to drop their makeshift weapons.

Panting and dishevelled, several men were singled out, and Abbot Bradford left Sir Tobias to speak with the bailiff.

A bad business all round Sir Tobias decided, as he turned back to the hostelry to collect his party. Mounted, they left Sherborne by skirting round what was left of the brawl, shielding Lady Alice, and rode through Newland thus joining their way home without having to go down Cheap Street. He was relieved to observe that the sight and sound of the trouble had not alarmed Alice; rather had lifted some of her lethargy.

Martin Cooper crouched in the doorway of his mother's deserted house. It was five weeks since he had met with Lady Alice and divulged Sir Allard's message - five rather disastrous weeks for him.

His mother had left with a pedlar a neighbour had told him, and had been gone six months. The house had been neglected and partially burnt by local youths. Martin had managed to save a few possessions and sleep fitfully in the shell of the downstairs room, but no-one would give him work in his condition, and he could see no future here. He was tired of the dirt and squalor of this life –there seemed no respite for him.....death would be welcome, but he favoured one final throw of the dice. He would try to return to Sherborne where he had received kindness, and seek out Sir Tobias to beg for help.

Martin was weakened by his injuries, as yet improperly healed, and by hunger. He had been forced to beg and steal for food and his disability made him slow and clumsy. His blinded eye sometimes tried to flicker into discerning light from dark, but his stump was still raw and inflamed.

He bound his few belongings together, gathered his makeshift crutches and made his way slowly and haltingly onto the main track leading to the West.

There was traffic along this road today; carts of vegetables, cookware, trinkets....he knew better than to beg for a lift, but one battered cart did stop and take pity on him, and the carter hoisted him up. He was going as far as Henstridge – luck at last – Henstridge was over half way there.

The cart was empty, the horse was old and slow and Martin lay in the back, oblivious of the rotting vegetable leaves under him. He dozed, thankful for the ride.

The carter put him down when they reached Henstridge and Martin took up his crutches and his shabby goods and began his walk.

He was not so fortunate this time. No-one stopped to offer lifts – indeed, traffic diminished as the day wore on.

By nightfall he had reached Milborne Port, and remembered that Purse Caundle was close by. Did he dare approach the home of Sir Tobias? Maybe it would be better to continue down into Sherborne and seek him there......it was less intrusive into the life of a family who had suffered such devastating news and he had no wish to distress the Lady Alice further with his unwelcome presence.

He needed to seek shelter for the night. Milborne Port was a large village with a guildhall, alehouses and several rows of dwelling places, some of which were clearly trading places as well. He had no coin, so he would have to seek a sheltered deserted doorway. He could go no further. – his stump ached, and his arms were stretched to the limit with the weight of his body supporting him on his crutches, and the difficulty of holding his belongings increased the problem. Several times he had considered throwing them into the ditch, but it seemed to him that to do so would be ditching his very self.

He settled in the corner of a burnt out house, sheltered partially from the night breeze which had sprung up. Hunger gnawed at him but there was no place from which to beg unless he dragged himself nearer to one of the ale houses. He wound his thin arms round his body to consolidate warmth, for although the day had been fine, the night air was chilly.

He slept intermittently throughout the night, waking now and then at the eerie sounds of moving animals and feeling cold every time he stirred. At day break he moved stiffly away from the place in which he had sheltered after relieving himself.

The track looked uninviting today. Cloud cover gave a grey hue to the landscape and Martin's desire to reach Sherborne faltered. What could he possibly expect Sir Tobias to do for him? He sank down on a low wall near the last small house in the village and looked about him. Milborne Port was a mixture of fine houses, shops – he could see a common bakehouse nearby – and a well. There were also several streets of poorer houses built closely together as in other towns and villages.

Martin edged closer to the bakehouse. His strength and resolve had ebbed away this morning. He was a broken man with little hope left. There was nothing and no-one for him – all events seemed against him.

He turned away, stumbling on the rough path and crashing to the ground unevenly. Pain from his stump shot through him, burning his flesh in its intensity and making him cry out involuntarily. His meagre crutches had clattered out of his reach. He dragged himself into a crouch, using his arms, and stretched out to attempt to reach them.

A hand that was not his put the crutch within his reach. He looked up. A young woman stood nearby, her uncooked dough in a crock ready to bake in the common bakehouse. She moved the second crutch nearer to him with her foot. He mumbled his thanks, and she turned to go into the bakehouse.

Martin struggled to get himself upright again, ridiculously encouraged by that one small act of kindness.

He retrieved his belongings from where they had fallen, and tucked the knobbly crutches underneath his armpits once again. His progress was slower today. His energy appeared to be totally spent. Each step was painful. He had long ago lost the shoes given to him, so his one sound foot was swathed in sacking, which had become dirty and threadbare. Indeed, strands of hemp were hanging from his foot, threatening to trip him up.

He paused at the very last house, leaning on a crumbling stone wall. The village was alive now, shop fronts opening up, village people beginning their day, goodwives chatting...he could hear animal sounds, children crying, whole fit healthy men going about their daily work. What was he? How could he hope to fit in? He closed his eyes. When he opened them again the young woman who had moved his crutches was standing beside him, looking curiously at him. She held her cooked loaf in her hand, fresh from the oven.

"Would you like some bead?" she asked.

Martin swallowed. He wanted to snatch at the bread but her loaf was quite small. She broke off a piece and handed it to him. He tried not to wolf it down but it was hard to swallow, so dry was his mouth.

The woman turned in to this last house, leaving Martin ashamed that he had not thanked her. Her door was still open, and Martin called after her.

"Thankyou, ma'am" he managed to croak.

She returned to close the door, carrying a young baby on her arm.

"You're welcome to rest by the wall for a while", she said.

Martin said nothing. He was wary of the wiles of women – where there was a baby there must be a husband. He had no wish to be pilloried for actions in which he had no part. However, in his need, he sank down gratefully, leaning back against the wall. The young woman went back inside the house and closed the door.

Davy, the serving man of Matthias Barton, had fulfilled his early morning chores at Barton Holding and using the nag, was ambling towards Lydia's cottage. Lydia was the young widow of his late friend Ben Glover, who had been murdered by bogus monks in the Abbey in the early Spring of last year. He and Matthias had worked with Sir Tobias to attempt to bring justice following more killings – the false monks had even made an attempt on Lydia's life by firing her house. She was now living in the last poor dwelling in the village, which Matthias had managed to procure for her. It was in questionable condition, but it was at least a roof over her head, and Davy and his wife Elizabeth provided her with whatever help they could. Lydia's child had been born just two days after the murder of her young husband, and even now, over a year after his murder, she found it difficult to find a way of forging new beginnings.

Today, Davy was bringing her some pottage from Elizabeth, who had deliberately made more than they needed. It would provide Lydia with two days of good meals. She had no other family members apart from an aging mother, so Lydia had been well cared for by Matthias' household. Davy was disturbed, on approaching Lydia's home, to see a crippled beggar lounging outside the house, with his back against the low wall edging Lydia's domain.

"What business do you have here?" he asked roughly, shaking the man by the shoulder. Martin roused himself – this must be the husband. He knew he should not have lingered.

"None, sir," he replied, "Your lady kindly offered me bread. I will be on my way directly."

"You will indeed," Davy retorted, firmly.

Martin reached for his crutches which were leaning against the wall, and propelled himself up painfully. His good eye took in the man facing him.....stocky build.... reddened cheeks which told of outdoor work....troubled blue eyes raking him up and down with honest suspicion. He had arrived by horseback...a simple nag...and was carrying a dish carefully wrapped.

Lydia opened the door at the sound of Davy's raised voice.

"Davy – don't be too harsh. This man has done nothing wrong. I offered him bread and rest. He just looked so tired."

Davy softened his voice, but was no less adamant.

"Lydia, some people are not all they seem. You must be careful. These are dangerous times. You are on your way, you said?" this last to Martin.

"I am bound for Sherborne. I seek the Coroner."

"And what business would you have with the Coroner? He lives near here – you'll not find him at Sherborne every day."

The futility of his mission almost overcame Martin once more. The tone of the man called Davy had implied that he could have no possible reason to have business with such as the Coroner, but Martin remembered the compassion shown to him by that household.

Davy took in the state of Martin.....thin..gaunt..deep shadows under his eyes....one eye damaged and unlovely to look at....a stump at the knee wrapped in some kind of cloth.....yet a fellow man in need of help....or perhaps a clever trickster....who could tell?

"Wait here until I deliver this dish to Lydia and see that all is well with her. My master knows the Coroner. I will take you to our home...my master can decide whether the Coroner should be informed."

And so, riding on the nag which Davy led, Martin Cooper arrived at Barton Holding.

Chapter 4

Matthias was perplexed by the arrival of Martin Cooper. He understood Lydia's need to be kind, but the appearance of Davy leading the nag with what appeared to be a bundle of rags on the saddle had shocked him from his normal calm.

He was afraid Davy may have been taken in by trickery, and was much more cautious in his approach than Davy had expected.

Martin stumbled as he dismounted, even his good leg seemed to have suffered cramps which prevented him from being dignified in any way.

He hated to be thought nothing more than a beggar, picked out of the dirt by the whim of a young woman.

Matthias directed Davy to take him through the kitchen to the little back room, where he would not be on display, for the scholars were still in session, then he was obliged to return to the schoolroom to continue his work, leaving Davy and Elizabeth to deal with Martin.

By the time the boys left, Martin had used the pump in the yard to clean himself, and yet again had been clothed by strangers. Elizabeth could see how exhausted he was, and dragged a straw filled paliasse into the barn.....and Martin slept uneasily while Davy recounted the strange meeting to Matthias.

"I need to wake him to talk with him," Matthias decided. "I cannot just call on Sir Tobias without some understanding of what he wants.......suppose he means him harm?"

Martin roused himself as soon as Matthias entered the barn. It was dark and cool, and Elizabeth had settled the paliasse in one corner. Davy remained outside, within calling distance, should Matthias need him.

"What is your business with the Coroner?"

" He helped me.... I had hoped he might help me again."

"In what way did he help you?

Martin's voice broke, and he covered his face with his hands.

"He and his Lady were kind......."

"How do you know Sir Tobias? How can I be sure you are not here to do him harm?"

"I was not always crippled as I am now....I was once of use to his son-in-law."

Matthias gasped. "You are the squire of Sir Allard?"

Martin nodded.

"I know of his trouble. You can speak freely....my man Davy does not yet know the full story. Tell me how we can help you."

Slowly and painfully, Martin told his tale. How he had intended to go home...try to help his mother understand his new state...perhaps find some menial chore he could do for a few coins, but the desertion of his mother and the partial burning of his house had left him feeling there was no place for him in his village. Neighbours were very much against his mother and her ways, and had offered him no assistance.

Remembering the kindness shown by the Coroner's household, despite the humiliating news he had brought them, he thought there might be some opening for him that Sir Tobias might know of....but now he was near, he realised that it was foolish and presumptuous.....

Matthias remembered well how useless and defeated he had felt when he had first fled abroad after the death of his parents and sisters. Their situation was different, but nevertheless, he had experienced deep despair and an overwhelming fear of the unknown... and he had not been as wounded as Martin...wounded in spirit, but not in a physical sense. Martin was wounded in both senses.

"Rest tonight, Martin, and tomorrow I will visit Sir Tobias on your behalf. They have had troubles of their own, as you must know. It may be wiser to sound the Coroner out before you see him. I will also send Elizabeth to visit the apothecary tomorrow...you need some salve on your eye and some better binding on your knee."

Martin ate with Davy and Elizabeth that evening, silently absorbing the peace of the kitchen. He said little to them of how he knew Sir Tobias, but Elizabeth drew him out a fraction on how he had managed to make the journey from Shaftesbury.

Davy found some better wood and sat quietly carving smoother handles for a different pair of crutches.

"Lend me your knife," Martin ventured, " I have some skill with wood...I think I can smooth them more perfectly at the top."

Davy cautiously handed over his knife, and Martin sat patiently whittling at the wood, smoothing it with his hands until it felt evenly curved. He tried it tentatively under one arm, and Davy watched with admiration as he saw that Martin did have a true feel for the wood.

Matthias gave William a message for Sir Tobias when the squire delivered Luke to school the next morning, and at the close of the afternoon, Sir Tobias rode over to collect Luke himself.

It troubled the Coroner that he could think of no suitable way at present to help Martin, and as he and Matthias sat in the now empty school room, he expressed admiration for Martin's tenacity in braving the journey in his weakened condition.

"I am at a loss this moment to know how best to help. We know nothing about him, we do not understand his interests or skills….the almshouses are hardly available to him as he is not a resident of Sherborne. He will simply be classed as a beggar among the many…. and he is hardly healed yet, either."

"Let me speak with Davy and Elizabeth," Matthias said, " the way forward for now is to offer him shelter and some peace to heal a little more. Perhaps then we can find some better help for him."

"That makes him one of the more fortunate pieces of debris from this failing war."

There was a bitter tinge to Sir Tobias' tone which hitherto had not been obvious. The glorious days of the fifth Henry were past. Sir Tobias remembered how still they had been before Agincourt, His Grace the King, mounted, riding calmly amongst the men, a word here, a word there. There were those who prayed and those who cursed and those whose fear made them vomit, but Sir Tobias had not been one of those.

There was strict discipline amongst those troops, waiting silently for the command to move forward. There was no hint of the chaos which Martin had described, although Sir Tobias was aware that after the battle, there was looting, but there was also order, imposed quite quickly once the injured had been carried in and the dead counted.

The death of His Grace had been a disaster for the ongoing war with France and so unexpected; who would have thought that the King would succumb to the bloody flux? But it had happened and his son Henry, a babe of nine months, had been declared King. Oh, his father had left a will in which he had made good provision for the kingdom...with John Duke of Bedford to have the regency of France. Bedford had done his best... but now he too had died after many years of unstinting service, and victories won by Henry were slipping away. The sixth Henry was certainly not made from the same cloth as his father.

Matthias knew he was thinking of the debris which had reached as far as his own family through Allard's desertion and the declining discipline of the English troops and was sorry it had touched his friend's family in such a way.

Davy and Elizabeth were nervous at first when Matthias called them into the schoolroom, and Sir Tobias did not need to tell them the details of his involvement with Martin; suffice to say Martin had brought news of Allard which had distressed the family. Eventually they would work it out for themselves.

"If he is such a man as myself," Davy began, hesitantly, "he would not want to be part of a charitable act. He must be offered work as well as shelter. The only other way is to issue him with an official licence to beg."

Matthias and Sir Tobias saw the logic of this.

"What work could you offer, Matthias?" Sir Tobias asked.

Matthias thought . "I don't rightly know what manner of man he is," he began, "so I could not say. Maybe he can read? Perhaps it would be best to offer him shelter initially and learn what he might best do – it could even be something in the village rather than in this house. This could just be his lodging for a while."

"That seems best," Elizabeth offered, shyly, "let him think he is coming here to be tended to in his need....we will ask the apothecary for salves and herbs and potions to ease his wounds. Then when the master has come to know him better, we can talk further of this."

"He appeared to have some skill with his hands...he handled the wood with care," Davy volunteered.

Sir Tobias found Martin in the barn, resting on the paliasse Elizabeth had made up for him.

"I am glad you found the courage to return, Martin. Before we find employment you must heal a little and regain some strength and health. Matthias has offered to oversee your needs while you heal, and Elizabeth has a little skill in caring...it is better for you to be here in Matthias' house where there will be more peace for you than in my household. When Matthias feels you are ready, we will talk again."

That night on his paliasse, Martin wept with gratitude.

Elizabeth was as good as her word; the next day she walked to the apothecary after first calling on Lydia. Her explanation of Martin's wounds was clear. She described his blinded eye, also adding that it seemed to Martin that sometimes he thought he could distinguish light from dark. She took account of the curiosity of people, and gave out that Martin was a friend of the Coroner's son-in-law and had been seriously wounded in battle, managing to make it as far as Sherborne.

Anthony Sewell, the apothecary, listened with interest as she supplied details of his amputation. He expressed wonder that infection had not set in, and set about pounding herbs and oils into pastes for her to apply to his raw stump, - for it was still raw, as Elizabeth had seen, although she could smell no infection.

"When he is rested, bring him to the shop, Mistress. There may be more we can do to assist the healing. I have used yarrow for his soreness and a wash of rue for his eyes, but I would like you to bring him to me for further infusions which may help."

Martin slipped into the routine of the household more easily than Matthias had expected. Davy and Elizabeth accepted his presence calmly, and the scholars hardly had occasion to see much of him. Davy made the barn more habitable for their guest, and the rest and peace which Martin experienced assisted his healing. He would never be free of his disability, but the crutches he had fashioned for himself were easier to operate, and he found the ache in his stump less by the week.

The cauterisation done by the camp surgeon had kept infection at bay. There was just the matter of rubbing and soreness.

His eye had flickered into life once or twice, and in time the swelling and inflammation had lessened, due in no small part to Elizabeth's insistence on using the potions given by Anthony Sewell.

Sir Tobias had visited him once, and expressed his pleasure at being able to help in some small way, but Matthias could sense that Martin was becoming restless.

"I need to move on, Master Barton," Martin said one evening as Summer drew to a close. "I am very grateful for all you have done to help me but I cannot be a passenger in your household for very much longer."

"Where will you go?" Martin asked, troubled by Martin's insistence.

"Maybe to Sherborne....I feel I know the town a little and people about have been very kind."

"Wait a little longer," Martin advised. "Lydia needs a cot for her child.She is growing out of her rush basket, and you have some skill with wood."

Davy took Martin to see Lydia to make arrangements for Martin to make a cot for the growing babe.

Lydia was too proud to accept a gift from him and had but sparse coin to spare for payment.

"Don't think of it as a gift," Martin told her, "rather my thanks for your kind actions which surely saved my life. I had all but given up on myself."

Martin called on her a couple of times to measure the child and the place where the cot would be positioned.

Once whilst he was there he mended the door frame so it was a better fit, allowing the latch to work more efficiently. Each time Lydia shared soup and bread with him to thank him for his work.

Both times he had walked to Lydia's house, using his crutches with more dexterity, despite the journey being slow.

By early September, the cot was finished, and Martin prepared to leave.

"Thank you, Martin. I shall miss making soup for two," Lydia said shyly, as she placed the finished cot in its place in the room and shook out thin blankets for the child. A frision of pleasure lit Martin's face at her words, but he knew he must move on.

As he approached Barton Holding, he could see Sir Tobias' horse tethered in the yard. He was glad, as it meant he could thank the Coroner for his kindness before finally leaving.

Davy met him at the door.

"Go straight in," he told Martin. There was concern in his eyes.

Sir Tobias was standing by the window with his back to the room. Martin could see there was unhappiness in his very stance, and Matthias looked up quickly as Martin entered tentatively.

The Coroner turned to face Martin.

"There is a young woman at my house, Martin. She claims to be Celeste. She tells me that far from deserting, Allard was mortally wounded and has died. She is demanding money from Alice. What light can you throw on this?"

Chapter 5

Martin's face blanched at Sir Tobias' words. Matthias watched him closely but could detect only puzzlement and shock.

"No sir," he declared, "Sir Allard and Celeste disappeared together whilst I was still in the surgeon's hands. He took his horse and all his belongings. He was definite in his intentions. I have not lied to you."

"The girl is as you described to me. She is unaware that you are here. She has a ring which belonged to Alice and which Alice gave to her husband before he left."

Matthias and Sir Tobias exchanged glances.

"Is this some trickery between you?" Matthias asked. "I find it hard to believe, but if this girl is really Celeste, whose tale is correct?"

"On my oath, sir." Martin began

Sir Tobias held up his hand for silence.

"Matters of the county I can deal with as justly as possible, but matters touching my own family I find hard to comprehend. Lady Alice has not seen the woman...and I hope to protect her from doing so, but I want this Celeste away from my home as soon as possible. I am not willing to pay her what she asks for the return of the ring until we have plumbed the depths of this strange, twisted tale."

Normally clear headed and rational, Sir Tobias felt weakened by this new development. His legs were shaking, his head would not clear, his emotions were in turmoil. He hoped the tremor in his voice had not been noticed.

"I am ready to leave this house, Sir Tobias," Martin began, but Sir Tobias interrupted him.

"No, Martin...until we have the truth of the matter, you will stay here. That is not an invitation...it is an order."

Matthias remained silent. He could not bring himself to think that Martin had deceived them all.....he had begun to like the young man and to have respect for the way in which he had arrived with news for Sir Tobias despite his injuries..... surely there was some way to discover the truth...but why would Celeste sail across the narrow sea and confront Sir Tobias if there was no truth in the matter.

" I order you to remain in the vicinity until we have investigated further. Matthias, will you allow Martin to remain here under these new circumstances?"

"I will," Matthias decided.

"Matthias, I want you to go over Martin's version of the events minutely...write down everything. Details matter."

Supper was a silent affair that evening. Martin felt shamed by the looks verging on puzzlement which passed between Elizabeth and Davy.

They spoke little to him of the girl, having agreed with Matthias not to speak of the affair until the scribing of the events were done. Conversation was stilted and general.

Before it became too dark to write, Matthias listed the events as Martin re-lived them.

Celeste had appeared well before Christmas. She was of French origin but had near perfect English.

Many of the men spoke French in a rough and ready way, and there had been much teasing between Celeste and the other girls about their ability to speak both English and French. She was lively and funny, clearly had some kind of education and seemed to come in and out of the camp at will. At first she was friendly and witty with all the men, but soon had fastened on Sir Allard who spent all his waking hours talking with her whenever possible, and soon after Christmas it was clear they had become lovers. Allard became careless of his duties to his men, and sometimes exhibited a cruel streak if he failed to get his own way, wanting the younger men to cover some of his duties. One or two of the younger men were resentful of Allard's relationship with the girl, believing that Allard had usurped their place in Celeste's attention. Martin had tried to pre-empt some of this, but not very successfully. He and Allard had become close friends, despite the difference in their station in life. Martin admitted that they would drink together, often late into the night before the coming of Celeste, and would share jokes, discussions on life and love and talk about their hopes for the future.

The only discussion after Celeste was concerning his desperate need to escape from the camp with Celeste... his infatuation grew by the day.

Celeste was aware that Sir Allard was married....this did not concern her one bit. Martin did not like her cold hearted attitude to Lady Alice but was reluctant to say so to Sir Allard, who suddenly made Martin feel the difference in their social standing.

Then came the disastrous events following the death of the Duke of Bedford, when the two warring factions of the French, The Burgundians and the Armagnacs, signed a peace treaty. This robbed the English of their Burgundian ally, and without this important support, the English were caught in a trap of never ending defeat.

Allard immediately resumed his responsibilities as Captain...caring for his injured men and carrying Martin to the camp surgeon for treatment. It was Allard, together with others, who had held Martin for his amputation and who had begged the surgeon to cauterize the wound before Martin bled to death. When he was sufficiently conscious to notice, Celeste and Allard had disappeared.

He had heard Celeste mention Paris several times, so it was possible that they had travelled there. Martin didn't think she had the air of a country girl, so Paris might seem to be correct. The English had retreated from Paris, leaving it a free city.

Allard had not been wounded in the skirmish...he had been on two feet, helping those of his men who had been unlucky enough to be in the line of fire. He had left no word of farewell to anyone. All Martin could say was that he had tried to dissuade him from this course of action when he had understood that Allard was contemplating it. He had been disappointed to discover that he had not been successful. From then on, Martin's world became a pain filled blur. His account ended abruptly there.

Matthias studied Martin as he sat uneasily in the darkening room. Despite the accusations of the girl, he met Matthias' eyes openly.

"Could I see Celeste?" Martin ventured.

"Did you like her?" Matthias asked him.

"No. She appeared to stir up aggression amongst some of the men," was the response. "At first she was very free with her sexual favours."

"And then latterly they were all reserved for Sir Allard?"

"Seemingly. Allard distanced me as the affair grew."

After Martin had retired to the barn, Matthias sought Davy and the two men sat together in the schoolroom by the light of a rush candle, for September was drawing on and the evenings were not so light. The afternoon had troubled Davy.

"Elizabeth and I had talked about asking you to allow Martin to keep the barn as a lodging and to try to set up work in the village with his skill in wood. I suppose you'll not consider it now?"

"It is still worth considering. I am not convinced that this Celeste is telling the truth, but why would she come here with no reason? Martin has asked if he can see her."

Matthias knew that Sir Tobias was bound to investigate the claims, and resolved to take Martin over to Purse Caundle to confront the girl.

Celeste had vowed to return the next day to press her claim on Sir Tobias and to try to see Lady Alice. She was bold faced and hard eyed, her golden curls tangled as though she had slept rough. Her finery was somehow tarnished. If this was what Allard had thrown his life away for, Sir Tobias was sorry – and surprised. There was none of the gaiety that Martin had described. Despite her bold front, she seemed to be less certain of herself on this second visit, as if it were all an effort.

Martin and Matthias arrived at the house as Celeste was preparing to leave after another stormy meeting with the Coroner. Martin had managed to mount the nag with help and some difficulty, but he was grateful for the opportunity to ride, and he controlled the docile nag with skill, despite his initial problems.

Celeste glanced at the two men arriving on horse-back and made to excuse herself with a flounce towards the gate. There was no sign of recognition as she edged past the nag.

Martin's voice rang out, shrill with shock and disbelief.

"This is not Celeste! This is not the woman Sir Allard left with!"

Matthias wheeled his horse round as Celeste quick-ened her pace. She glanced over her shoulder to see who had spoken and spat in Martin's direction.

"Liar! You were not there!" she hissed.

"Neither were you," Martin rejoined, as Matthias put a hand on her shoulder to detain her. She bit his hand, drawing blood, but Matthias held firm as William hurried out to bring the girl back.

After an initial struggle she allowed herself to be led back to Sir Tobias, but her hard eyes blazed with fury as she spat out her story again.

"This man is deranged with his injuries," she said, hatefully - "he is a nothing. A nobody. Why should we believe him?"

Martin stood as straight as he was able on his crutches, which had been strapped to the side of his saddle.

"This is not Celeste," he repeated.

"Crippled in mind as well as in body," retorted the girl, tossing her tangled hair back from her face.

"Show him the ring you took from Sir Allard," Sir Tobias commanded her. She fumbled in her bodice, a sly look overtaking her face as she revealed more than was necessary of her well rounded breasts.

"There!" she cried, opening her palm. The ring lay there, a single gold band with a simple gem stone,

Allard's initials clearly visible etched into the side. Unmistakably it was the ring Martin had noticed often on Sir Allard's finger.

"I believe that to be Sir Allard's ring," he admitted, looking curiously at the girl standing before him, her bosom heaving with tension, "but this is not Allard's woman. She is nothing like her."

"Who is this man?" demanded Sir Tobias of her, indicating Martin. She scornfully abraided him.

"A man from the camp," she replied, "wounded beyond any woman's desire – intent only on mischief to satisfy his unfulfilled lust." Her lip curled with disgust as she took in the extent of his injuries.

"He cannot even see me properly – why should he challenge me – I have travelled far to claim some recompense for Allard's death. I will not be denied it by a cripple intent only on vicarious revenge for his injuries."

Martin cringed at her harsh words. She gave them a ring of authority, and his new found inner confidence was shattered at her cruelty.

"Martin sees pretty well with one eye, mistress" Matthias commented, irritated by her tone and choice of words. Watching her closely, he observed a certain nervous tension in her body, a wariness which was not apparent before.

"Tell me, where were you when men were injured and brought to the surgeon?"

The sly look returned to the girl's eyes.

"I had no part in their battle. I was elsewhere."

"And why come to Sir Allard's father in law? Why not to his father?"

"And where is Sir Allard's horse and his posses-sions?" Sir Tobias asked her.

"Taken by his friends," was the answer, less convinc-ing this time.

"No!" burst from Martin. " He was gone with his horse and possessions and the girl Celeste – not this girl!"

There was passion and conviction in his words. Sudden hatred blazed in the girl's eyes.

"You – who are you? What are you doing here?"

"I was squire to Sir Allard – and you are not Celeste." Some of the bravado drained from the girl.

"The man Allard is dead," she said, flatly, "I was sent to claim some money on Celeste's behalf."

"There is no money to be had without proof of my son in law's death," Sir Tobias told her, " and any money will come from Sir Alwyn, not from me."

The girl was sent on her way with instructions never to return with such a story, and the men gathered to reflect.

"I do not like this tale," Sir Tobias decided. "Perhaps I should have detained her, but that was certainly Allard's ring. I had no reason to prevent her from going." He felt great unease as he spoke.

"The girl was nothing like Celeste. She had not the bearing or the glossiness of complexion. Celeste was quite beautiful – very vibrant. She was of French extraction and wore her vibrance in every part of her person."

"That sounded quite poetic, Martin," Matthias said.

Martin smiled ruefully. "That was how she affected the men. She brought life and gaiety into a soldier's world – it's a world of boredom, tedium, grime –she lit it up – and her friends, too."

"Her friends? The girl was not, perhaps, one of her friends, unnoticed by you?"

"No, the friends all disappeared once Celeste had caught Allard's heart."

There was silence as the picture grew in their minds.

"Do you think Allard is dead? William asked.

Sir Tobias frowned.

"We need to discover the truth of that. Martin, are you sure he didn't die of wounds received after you had been taken to the surgeon?"

"I am as sure as I can be," Martin replied.

Sir Tobias refilled their goblets, listening to Martin's account.

"Once the initial hail of arrows was over, there was no more fighting. It was not a major battle, more a frustrated firing of weapons. I was unlucky to have been caught in the cross stream. When I was returned to camp the men were in disarray. Sir Allard had gone, they told me. He had left after dark with his horse – the men were angry and disappointed in him. They didn't know how to organize themselves. A couple just slipped away the next night – we never knew what happened to them. Several had been wounded or killed, and the rest wandered helplessly around until they found some other men to serve who needed them. Allard's going produced chaos for a while in the group."

Sir Tobias found the account disturbing. It spoke of weakening discipline and organization among the troops, and he could well imagine the sense of betrayal when the men woke to find their captain gone.

"Martin, - I do believe this girl is not Celeste, but this leads to a deeper mystery. She has been put up to this by other people – people who have known Sir Allard. They did not expect you to be here – if you had not been present, I would not have known this claim to be fraudulent. When you appeared and failed to recognize her, it put a whole new angle on this."

"What has happened to Sir Allard?" William asked.

It was a question that was puzzling them all.

"Clearly something bad," Matthias said, "and what of the real Celeste? Is she too dead, or did someone betray him- was he murdered for his treachery?"

"We need to discover the detail," Sir Tobias decided. "We must travel to the source, which appears to be Calais. William, will you go for me, travel to the Calais camp and root out the men who served Allard? Matthias, I wish you were free to go with William. This is too close to my heart for me to be involved, not to mention the responsibilities I have in England. Would you consider accompanying William?"

He spoke hesitantly, aware that Matthias had responsibilities to his scholars, but also needing to use Matthias' quick brain power.

"It would be very difficult," Matthias began, "the school relies on my presence – Davy cannot teach the boys..."

"But Alice can....with Davy's help. Alice can read... and teach, especially if Martin would stay to help?"

Martin was as much taken by surprise at the suggestion as Matthias was.

"I can read, and I am willing to be present with the Lady Alice and work under her direction if she will have me," he said slowly, watching Matthias as he spoke.

Matthias frowned, playing with his father's ring on his finger. His life was once again taking a new and unplanned turn. He was enjoying his school; the scholars respected him, were learning fast. How would Alice cope? How much help would Martin really be able to give her - if indeed she would agree to work with him, and more importantly, how would the merchant clients, the fathers who paid the fees, regard his absence and a woman in his place?

He voiced his concerns tentatively. Sir Tobias frowned, scratching distractedly at a mark on the table in front of him. He refilled their goblets.

"I should have detained the girl to question her further," he said, "this whole incident is too personal – it threw my equilibrium. Anyone less connected to my family and I would have been thinking more clearly."

"She has not long left," William ventured. "I can ride after her and bring her back."

It was agreed that William would do so, and he left immediately.

This gave Matthias time to ponder over the suggestion that he should leave his school to Lady Alice for a while and travel to Calais with William. After an hour or so, William returned reporting a fruitless search; the girl had vanished. William was surprised, for she had left on foot with no sign of a horse or an accomplice, as far as he could tell.

Sir Tobias was annoyed with himself for allowing the girl to leave without further questioning, and it was decided that he and William would go into Sherborne the following day to search for her.

"That assumes she came from Sherborne and returned there," Matthias pointed out. "She may well have been brought from further afield."

Whilst the two men searched Sherborne for the girl, Matthias wrestled with his own dilemma. How would Lady Alice take to the idea of being asked to teach his pupils?

More importantly, how would the families of his pupils react to his absence? Should he refuse to go? Somehow, he did not feel comfortable refusing Sir Tobias.

On their return from Sherborne, Sir Tobias had to report that no-one could swear to having seen such a girl. She had apparently disappeared.

Matthias was forced into a decision, and late that afternoon, he visited Alice with Lady Bridget. She had recently returned to her own home, a small lodge house in the grounds of Sir Tobias' demesne.

"Let me have the telling of the tale," Lady Bridget offered, "I know Alice's reactions well."

They were admitted to the lodge house by a maid servant. Alice was in her solar. She stood up in surprise as Lady Bridget and Matthias were shown in by the girl. They were served refreshment, and made light conversation, but Alice's guarded eyes told them that she expected more.

"Alice, we have called with a strange story," Lady Bridget began. "Please hear me out with patience. Your father had a visit yesterday from a stranger, a girl. She called herself Celeste. She returned again today."

Matthias glanced at Alice. She rose to her feet as if to leave. Her face had paled, her lips tightened. Lady Bridget continued more gently, but was determined to tell the tale distinctly and swiftly.

"She was in possession of a ring which I believe you gave Allard before he left. She demanded money for its return and told us that the man Martin had lied, and that Allard was in fact slain in battle."

Alice cried out involuntarily and would have fallen had Matthias not steadied her by the elbow. He lowered her to a chair. Her eyes were black with shock and her face was white, drawn and suddenly older.

Lady Bridget continued, "Listen carefully, Alice. Martin arrived and saw this girl. She is not Celeste. She was sent to extract money from your father – or maybe you. However, we need to find out what has really happened to Allard. Is he alive or is he dead? Did he desert of was he wounded? Your father has asked William and Matthias to travel to Calais and find out the truth."

Alice was perfectly still for a few moments, trying to repossess herself.

"How can we be sure Martin is telling the truth?" she whispered, hoarsely.

The room seemed to swirl around her until she became conscious of Matthias' hand on her elbow. She shook it off impatiently.

"His testimony is without guile, Alice. It was from the heart, and furthermore, the girl did not recognize Martin – she had no idea who he was, and her story was broken when she learned that Martin had been Allard's squire. It was only then that she revealed that she had been sent by others to extract money. Whoever was behind this cruel affair could not have expected or even known that Martin would try to reach you to tell you of Allard's decision – he had been terribly wounded. It was Martin's own wish to speak with you. They were not expecting that. The girl has left." Matthias told her.

"Father let her leave?" Alice was clearly amazed.

"To his regret, yes. There was no trace of her. William rode after her, but she had vanished. Your Father and

William have just returned from Sherborne where they made several enquiries, but no-one had seen her."

Alice gazed from one to the other of them, her senses clearing.

"Why has Matthias come here, Mother?"

"Your father has asked me to travel to France with William to discover what has happened to Sir Allard," Matthias explained. His eyes never left her face, but his arm felt burned where she had shrugged him away.

"As you know, I cannot leave my scholars without a teacher. It is a newly started venture. Your father suggested that you would be able to teach them in my absence." He swallowed hard, uneasy about her decision. She had not looked kindly on him since the news of her husband's desertion.

Alice remained silent. It was hard to describe her feelings, even to herself. News had been brought by Martin at the end of July. It was now the end of September. Alice had lived with news of Allard's desertion for two months. During that time she had felt despair, rejection, sadness, anger, loss of hope for both herself and her son, but now just sadness with a slowly dawning realization that whilst Allard lived, she could never be a wife again and must rebuild for herself and her son.

"Would your man Davy be on hand for discipline if need be?" It was a leaning towards an answer.

"Davy is unlettered, but yes, he would be around. We hoped you might accept Martin as your help. He is lettered and has a degree of skill, despite his injuries. He is healing in both body and spirit and manages his crutches well."

"How long might you be absent?"

"William hopes no more than a week or two at the most."

Matthias would have liked to add that he hoped the experience would heal Alice in spirit, too – but her impatient shrug had warned him to stay silent.

Alice reluctantly agreed to call on Matthias the following day with her maid servant in attendance to observe the scholars in action..

For Alice, it might be a new beginning, but Matthias felt a return of the old enemy of despair and uncertainty.

Lady Alice arrived in the schoolroom with Luke and her serving maid the next morning. Martin greeted her courteously and she him, although somewhat coldly.

She watched as Matthias moved around the schoolroom, instructing, correcting, talking quietly and praising frequently the efforts of his young pupils. Luke enjoyed his mother looking over his work, and Martin observed quietly from the side-lines.

"I have been fortunate in these boys," Matthias told Alice and Martin a little later. "They are all obedient and respectful – a little in awe of me – don't make the mistake of trying to be their friend. You are their teacher. You must expect and demand respect. Equally, you must respect their efforts. They are all sons of local merchants. They started with nothing in the way of learning – or almost nothing. I have concentrated on basic number and simple letters. They have made progress. Copying letters is a good exercise - rewarded later with a story - I am using tales of the Greek heroes - and some outdoor play for a short while is good - it releases pent up energy."

It was the longest speech Matthias had made in Alice's presence, and he was so passionate about his school that he was able to talk with her normally for once, without the silly schoolboy blush. She, for her part, listened and appreciated his passion.

"We will do our best," she said, quietly, glancing at Martin. Martin nodded in agreement. He was overwhelmed but had taken in the orderliness and quiet of the schoolroom. The boys had looked at him curiously to start with but Matthias had told them how Martin had been wounded, and a feeling of awe overtook them as they understood that Martin had seen battle, endured pain and had emerged from it.

So it was decided. William and Matthias would depart from Poole the next day, and Lady Alice, assisted by Martin, would teach in Matthias' place until they returned.

Matthias hoped the journey would bring some peace to Lady Alice, and leave Martin's name unblemished.

Chapter 6

Matthias and William left for France as planned. September was drawing to a close, and Sir Tobias was anxious for the matter to reach a conclusion, added to which, once October and November arrived, the narrow sea crossing would be both dangerous and unpleasant.

Both men were reasonable sailors and they had no difficulty in obtaining a passage on a cog bound for Calais. They stabled their horses in Poole, intent on hiring horses in France, and once aboard, William settled down on deck wrapped in his great cloak, whilst Matthias sought out a couple of sailors, part of the crew. One of them, he learned, had crossed sometimes to Melcombe. He did remember bringing wounded men home as well as bringing other cargo. Matthias tried to describe Martin in as much detail as he could, but the crewman was unable to be certain that Martin was one of the injured. He thought he recalled an amputee, but he was so vague that Matthias gave up as he didn't want to put words into his mouth. He wondered why he was doubting Martin's story of his return to England, but it seemed wise to check as much of every aspect of the story as possible. After a short while, he gave the men some coin for their trouble and went to join William.

The wind was favourable and the cog was sturdy; it was late September when they arrived in Calais. William knew where to hire reliable horses, and after doing so, they headed for a hostelry where he had stayed before when on business for Sir Tobias.

Customers were varied, they discovered, as they dined on a tolerable dish of heavily spiced beef with root vegetables. There were several merchants, a sailor or two, and later on, a smattering of soldiers wearing the livery of Richard of York.

Matthias and William joined the latter with their own wine as darkness fell.

"I am searching for a man," Matthias began, "he was a captain under Duke Humphrey last year, and then seems to have become embroiled in the aftermath of the Burgundian withdrawal."

The soldiers, laughed, harshly, bitterly, Matthias thought.

"A thankless task - some dead - some wounded - some even deserted. The immediate fallout was vicious."

"His name?" the older soldier asked

"Sir Allard de Bhun"

"Where last seen?"

"After returning his men to the camp in Calais"

"We're returning to camp shortly. Do you have horses? There are a couple of men who joined us after their captain deserted."

Neither Matthias nor William admitted to looking for a man who had possibly deserted – it might well bring disaster on their heads.

They mounted and followed the men through the darkness. William was glad of his war belt, and Matthias was armed with his dagger, nervous now as the soldiers quickened their pace.

The camp was a sprawling, muddy affair – tents and pavilions giving it an appearance of a small tented city.

Torches flared at various intervals, revealing groups of men squatting round fires, eating, drinking, brawling. Once or twice, women could be glimpsed cavorting with soldiers who seemed to be very free with their hands, drunkenly leering down semi-naked breasts. After a while, they dismounted and followed their guide to a camp fire, circled by some six or seven men.

The soldiers who had brought them here left abruptly with a short bark saying, "These men might help you" and then disappearing into the darkness.

Matthias stepped forward into the firelight.

The men were unshaven and looked bored. They had drunk deeply.

"We are seeking news of Allard de Bhun" William began.

One of the men spat into the fire.

"You'll not find him here. He's gone."

"Were you one of his men?" Matthias asked

"Once. He betrayed us and left with his leman."

"How sure can you be?"

"He was our captain. He was spooked by the woman. She wouldn't leave him alone. He was besotted."

There was bitterness in the man's words.

"Do you know where they went?" The man shrugged and spat again.

Another spoke up. "I went with Celeste once. She was free with her favours until her hooks ensnared Sir Allard. I think they were making for Paris."

"What was Celeste like?" William asked.

"A clever bitch....Allard had class, and once she got him that was that. He changed. Didn't care any more."

The subject was closed to them. They didn't know any more and didn't want to discuss it any further, but one of the men called after them as they turned away,

"How come you know him?"

Matthias returned and explained that Martin, his squire, had reached them. They seemed more interested in that than in Sir Allard's wherabouts.

"Good man, that Martin. Looked after Sir Allard well. Glad he made it home. Thought he was done for."

"Sir Allard didn't deserve him – he wasn't so friendly with him once Celeste made her move – treated him more like an underling."

"Carried him in, though, when he was wounded – I saw him carried to the surgeon..."

There was no more talk and the men returned to their dice and drink.

They had lost their guides to return them to their hostelry and Matthias found the streets threatening and unfriendly. William was a solid presence, and kept resolutely to the centre of the narrow streets, and after taking several wrong turns, the lights of their inn came into view.

"So it appears Sir Allard really did desert," Matthias mused.

"Do we go to Paris?" William pondered, considering the journey, the hostilities and the sheer difficulty of searching for one Englishman amongst a city with no leads to help them.

Matthias tried to think as Sir Tobias would have wished.

"We will return home with only the information that Allard did desert. We cannot tell whether he is dead or alive."

"Yet to continue to Paris with only a possibility that he may have gone there seems futile," William volunteered.

The two men fought to reach the right decision.

"It will take us three days to reach Paris," William countered, "and Paris is large. Parts of it are dangerous, especially for Englishmen at present. Some hostelries are friendly towards us, needing the chinks, - others are treacherously bad. They cannot forget that the English occupied Paris until quite recently. There may be one or two Englishmen still living in the city, but there is hostility everywhere and we will need to be very cautious."

"We need someone with a more detailed knowledge of where someone like Allard and Celeste would be able to go," Matthias mused. "William, you have seen service for Sir Tobias before in this country. Who do you know who could help us?"

"I have an old acquaintance married to a French woman. We were in combat together. The last I heard he was living in Honfleur. He is unlikely to have news of Sir Allard, but he may be able to give me some advice on how things stand in Paris and whom to ask for lodgings. As we have already said, the English relinquished control of Paris last year – there will be some Englishmen who chose to settle there. From them we may learn more."

Matthias elected to stay in Calais, hoping for further leads there, whilst William rode to Honfleur to seek his one time acquaintance, Simon. He expected to be away two days.

During his absence, Matthias fretted about his own absence from his school, wondered how Alice was managing and hoped she was being kinder to Martin than she had appeared.

Although he wandered the streets and alleys during his wait for William, he discovered nothing that would give them any information. He marvelled at the sea trade coming in and out of the port, at the lively trade in the fish market as the catch was landed, and at the streets where he heard sailors swearing oaths he hadn't heard for some time, and in different languages, filled with more colour and noise than his own tiny backwater in England. He wished he felt confident enough to buy some gee-gaw for Lady Alice, but he was afraid it would be rejected, so he kept his silver in his purse.

The presence of soldiers in and out of the camp was of no help to him, and he was relieved when William returned, weary but with a slender thread of information.

"I have an introduction to a cousin of Simon's," he told Matthias. "She lives with her husband near the St. Denis area. We should go as travellers to the St. Denis festival – it's held on October 8th. The streets will be full...- everybody celebrates. If there are any other Englishmen there we will strike up a conversation with them."

Matthias was dismayed at the timing – he had not intended to be away so long, but he was unwilling to return home with no information.

It took four days to reach Paris. The road was wet in places, the villages hostile and the Autumn weather had become variable, one day chilly and windy, the next with patchy sun which still held a little late warmth.

They were dishevelled and tired when they reached the outskirts of Paris.

The city from a distance in the low evening sun was a shimmering visage of shining spires and towers encompassed by stout grey walls. As they drew nearer to the gates the shimmering image looked less inviting, and the grey walls were forbidding. William drew out his letter of introduction to prove his identity.

The warden at the St Denis gate spat disdainfully but let them pass. Once inside they were engulfed by the sights and smells of a vibrant, sour smelling, pulsating welter of humanity.

It was easier to lead their horses here rather than ride them, for where they had entered the streets were extremely narrow. A carriage could not have passed this way, and the houses, mostly timber, were overhanging, shutting out the light. A leat ran down the middle of the street, carrying away night soil and other garbage.

Commerce was still in progress and street cries assailed their ears; as they walked they had to beware of garbage and waste from market stalls under their feet, and everyone seemed to be in such a hurry. The noise of traders vying with each other for trade was deafening, and Matthias noticed that some traders actually went from door to door, displaying their wares to customers.

The street widened soon into an open square, and here the houses were taller and stone built, rising to three storeys. The streets became more generous and rather prosperous looking. An array of the populace threaded their way through the thoroughfares, adding colour and interest; there were wealthy merchants in costly velvet or woollen gowns, trimmed with fur according to their social standing, fine ladies with elaborate head dresses and full skirts as well as artesan workmen with doublet and hose, some of them carrying the tools of their trade. Knights in the livery of their lord swaggered through the streets and there seemed to be a beggar on every street turning, whining for alms.

William looked at his letter of introduction and headed into a narrower turning off the square. River smells began to invade their senses – the centre of Paris was built around the Ile de la cite, on the river Seine, which itself was a convergence of three rivers, the Seine being the largest.

Rue St. Denis was a wide boulevard running from the gate from which they had entered. William examined his letter of introduction carefully again and studied the narrow houses crammed into the street. They turned off the wider, sweeter smelling Rue St. Denis, and were now in a far darker place, the houses veering out into the space above their heads, nearly meeting.

William selected the house carefully and raised the door knocker, letting it connect with the door gently, to avoid any sense of aggression. Both men were aware that the English had occupied Paris until last year, and that their young and as yet untried young king Henry VI had been crowned in Paris only six years ago. Caution was a necessity.

The door opened a crack, and Matthias had the impression that the woman he saw showed more than a little fear. William introduced themselves, asked for M'sieur Robarte, and they waited in the dark hallway, listening to the whispered conversation.

After what seemed to be an inordinately long time, Guy Robarte himself appeared. He was a short, swarthy fellow, some forty years of age, clothed soberly as a scholar.

William offered him the letter with which Simon had provided him. His face cleared as he read it.

"You've seen my wife's cousin? Is he well?"

This was a friendly introductory gambit, during which his wife joined them, asking eagerly for news of her family, and her fearful apprehensive look had disappeared.

"There has been some ill feeling towards the few English people who have chosen to remain here," Guy Robarte explained as they nibbled on marchpane and relaxed with wine in Guy's well lit solar. Despite the narrow appearance of the road and the forbidding look of the tall house, crammed as it was beside others, the furnishings inside were comfortable and Guy had several well thumbed books lining one wall.

He was a scholar with a philosophical attitude towards the continuing politics between England and France, but Martha, his wife, was clearly nervous of repercussions against her, as an English woman. They talked briefly of such things before William felt it time to reveal their mission.

"There is a coven of students who infiltrate places where English soldiers frequent," Guy told them after their story was told, frowning as he remembered snatches of overheard conversations from his students.

"…but as far away as Calais?" Matthias exclaimed. "It has taken us four days to reach here!"

"Resentment of the English presence in Paris is high in student quarters," Guy explained, "It is not impossible to imagine a deliberate infiltration of young women deployed to lure soldiers away from camp – and to torture and kill them."

"…but this Celeste was purporting to adore Allard," Matthias protested, "…and surely one soldier…"

66

"One soldier...then another by a different woman in a different place in the camp... all soldiers of rank...but you may be right ...it could have been genuine affection."

"But you don't sound convinced?"

"Students here are young, hot bloodied, revengeful... and very patriotic - they see it as their duty to do whatever they can to disrupt the hated English occupiers,"

Guy's words were bleak. Matthias suddenly felt cold. Martha, who had said little, shivered.

"Are you not afeared?" Matthias asked her.

He thought of the peaceful country area around Milborne Port – even Sherborne, with its problems concerning the Abbot, and longed to return.

"No, I'm nervous, but not afeared. I've lived here with Guy for ten years, I am well known, but I keep my own counsel. I am happy in my house and in my husband."

"Sir Allard's squire thought Celeste lived in Paris," William told them. "He left Calais with his horse and possessions whilst Martin, his squire, was recovering from an amputation."

"I have no information to offer you," said Guy, with genuine regret, "but I can offer you accommodation while you seek other leads – you will need to move round the university quarter and the places where students frequent – their eating and drinking places... listen but take care... you are English."

Matthias was very mindful of his lack of concentration when he had been trying to follow suspects in Sherborne the previous year so he tried to forget his concern for the school and his desire to return home; he needed to be alert to snatches of loose talk – the sooner they had something of value, the sooner they could return to Calais and take ship.

"Tomorrow is the festival of St. Denis," Martha told them, "There will be students and apprentices on the streets as well as many others enjoying the festivities. You may be lucky enough to learn or see something to help you."

"Will you go with us?" Matthias asked her, on impulse.

She shook her head. "No, - I don't invite trouble...I'm happy enough here."

St Denis Day dawned fair with a cool breeze but a clear sky. Matthias and William chose to follow the procession from the Montagne Sainte-Genevieve on the left bank of the Seine, for there were many students and members of the faculty of the university here. Guy, as a member of a university faculty, was required to be part of the colourful and noisy procession, and Matthias and William were more than content to mingle with the crowd once they had navigated the long walk from St Denis to the Sorbonne. There were two important processions on this day which greatly increased the crowds in the street; the other concerned the bishops and decorated clergy and started at the opposite end of the city but Matthias and William followed Guy's advice and chose to mingle with the crowds in the student quarter. Guy thought this would be the better chance of gleaning information of any value.

Wood smoke wafted through the air at intervals as groups of citizens celebrated their day's holiday with cooked morsels of meat. A holiday aura fell over them as Matthias purchased some bread, but it was of poor quality for grain had been rationed severely during the

English occupation and the harvests had not yet sufficiently recovered. The pork slice William had purchased
was far more appetising.

They paused on the Pont St. Michel, somewhat
despondently, for they had seen or heard nothing to
help them. A group of students were sprawled on the
ground, partially blocking their way. They had drunk
deeply and were disputing fiercely the talents of prosti-
tutes, describing their specialities and bragging about
their successes with them.

"The best of all was Celeste," Matthias heard one of
them say, as he and William were preparing to push
their way past them.

"Well, she's gone." His friend told him, flatly. "Haven't
seen her since she flitted from Calais with her prize."

Matthias leaned on the parapet of the bridge and
forced himself into their conversation.

"Where do you find a good one?" he leered, hoping
he sounded coarse enough.

"You occupied our city- don't occupy our women,"
one of the students warned him, recognizing him from
his accent - but it was not unfriendly – more like student
riposte.

"Find them anywhere. They're rife…"said another.

"..but a good one…with specialities…" Matthias
persisted, afraid of losing this one slender thread they
had found.

"Don't you get good ones in England then?" one of
them jeered.

"The best ones are Italian," Matthias told him, and
enjoyed the look on their faces when he elaborated.
They looked at him after that with something like
respect.

William continued to lean on the bridge, gazing into the flowing river as though he had nothing to do with this ribald conversation. He thought Matthias was doing remarkably well.

"Celeste had her own little crowd of girls," the one who had first spoken said, rather sadly.

"The girls are still around," another volunteered, "but they're just not the same now Celeste has gone."

"Where did she go?" Matthias asked, innocently, careful to put no urgency of expression in his tone.

"Into the river," one told him, rather more drunk than the rest of them.

The party of students drew back from their loose mouthed friend.

"Hush – we don't know that for sure."

"Why into the river?" Matthias persisted.

"She'd gone off with an English soldier. The monseigneur didn't like that."

"These girls sound fun," Matthias said quickly, before the group could leave,

"Where can I find them?"

But the students had fallen silent. Their drunken friend had said too much. They stood him up between them and in various stages of disarray, moved rapidly on.

"I need to find these girls." Matthias decided.

Finding Celeste's girls was now priority number one.

Matthias went on alone, feeling William might be a hindrance. He waited until dusk and with remnants of the festival filling the street with danger, noise and smells, he moved towards the river and over the bridge onto the right bank.

Slatterns sat in doorways here, watchful pimps half hidden. Matthias assumed the air of a man seeking pleasure. He wasn't interested in these unkempt, unwashed girls, offering their bodies for a few centimes. He was in pursuit of Celeste's girls.

He had his purse on the usual cord round his waist, but he kept one hand firmly on it, for he knew he would need the contents to trade for information.

Some time later, his wanderings took him to the vicinity of Rue St. Denis, back across the river, which had been recommended to him as a place where he might find girls of quality. He was surprised, because that was near the area in which Guy lived, and where he had left William.

However, his informant had been correct. He found the darkness of the street intimidating; streets were not lit, but as this had been a celebration day there were still glimmers of light from hostelries and one or two outside fires giving off savoury smells of grilling meat now burnt to a cinder, which made his mouth water.

A girl emerged from the shadow of the house on the corner.

"Monsieur....do you seek company?"

She was attractive, sleek, well groomed. Where had she come from, Matthias wondered. He had seen no-one in the street...she had just appeared from the darkness.

"Possibly," he replied, "are you thirsty?"

She laughed, her voice low and throaty.

"For what?"

"For wine, first of all."

She led the way to a well set-up tavern on the main thoroughfare. It was clean and well lit. Several heads turned as they entered and Matthias felt scrutinized.

He ordered wine, and the girl sat close to him. He could feel her warmth...smell her profession.

She was fair haired, with widely set blue eyes and a mouth which looked as if it could pout meanly if refused her desires, but which at the moment was smiling at him over the rim of her goblet. Her dress was cut lower than Matthias had first thought and as she laid a hand on his knee and moved closer, he realised that she had arranged her dress deliberately to expose her breast at its most provocative.

"I have a select room, monsieur. Are you English?"

Matthias gazed at her, holding her eyes for a moment before she dropped them with false demureness.

"Do you know where I can find Celeste?" he murmured into her ear.

She removed her hand from his knee, her smile fading.

"Do you not feel the need for my services?" she asked, archly, deftly avoiding his questions and recovering her composure.

Matthias was accustomed to answering ladies with courtesy; he placed one hand over hers on the table and stroked it carefully with his thumb.

"Have you ever been to Calais?" he asked her, softly.

"Why Calais, monsieur? We are in Paris."

"Is Celeste in Paris?"

"Who is this Celeste?"

"I think you know;" he gambled on his intuition.

"Celeste has left," she murmured, moving his hand onto her thigh.

Matthias carefully moved his hand back to the table and placed a coin beside it.

"Celeste," he said, coolly, "Where is she?"

"She stepped outside the Circle," the girl answered, softly. Matthias smelled her fear as she stroked his thigh and moved her head closer to him. He added another coin.

"Monseigneur was not pleased."

Another coin appeared.

"She could not swim."

Matthias swallowed hard.

"So my fellow countryman, Allard, - where is he?"

The girl smiled sweetly at him but did not reply. Instead she raised her voice a little and said clearly,

"Monsieur...I couldn't allow you to take me like that! Whatever you do in places of ease in England it will not do here," and she dimpled prettily at him as a tall elegant Frenchman appeared behind Matthias.

The money he had put on the table had gone, and a wary look crossed her face.

"Shall we go monsieur?"

She took him by the hand with some urgency, raised him up, slipped her arm round his waist and nestled in towards him. Matthias sensed her urgency was not sexual but driven by fear. He allowed himself to be taken up a short flight of stone steps to a balcony over-looking the street. There was a two seater couch, plumply cushioned and a small ornate table with a jug of claret and two glasses.

"Please play the part," she whispered, pulling the laces of her bodice loose, and guiding Matthias' hands to her breasts.

He was ashamed to find her body aroused him, her obvious fear increasing his desire.

A shadow on the stair-well forced him to fumble at her bodice, opening it and cupping one warm breast in his hand. She sought his mouth with hers and soft lips pressed against his own, forcing him to reciprocate. She moved her hands against his body increasing his need still further. An unwilling involuntary groan escaped him.....it had been so long...the girl ran her hand lightly over his thighs, feeling his excitement. He attempted half heartedly to pull away, fearful of a trap, but her hands were insistent as she unfastened his points and continued her caressing.

It was over all too soon, as he had known it would be, but the girl was not at all disturbed and as she slipped her bodice back on, she glanced towards the stairwell. The shadow had gone.

"The Englishman was killed," she whispered. "Celeste was punished for her disloyalty – it was not part of the plan that she should fall in love."

Matthias adjusted his clothing and opened his purse.

"I'm sorry," he said, "I did not intend that to happen. Thank you for the information."

She looked over her shoulder again. The shadow had returned.

"A splendid performance, monsieur," she declared clearly, "you can find me again whenever you like."

Matthias stood up and the shadow disappeared, but he heard stealthy footsteps descend the stairwell and the clink of steel.

Money changed hands for the last time, and Matthias left her.

Chapter 7

Matthias chose not to disclose to William how he had obtained his information, and William's decision was that they should now leave for home. He could see no profit in lingering in Paris.....there was obviously a ring of students controlled by a senior personage deliberately targeting English soldiers but William felt there was nothing they could do about it.. that had not been their brief. They did, however, tell Guy Robarte about a cohort of girls controlled by a Frenchman infiltrating the English camp at Calais, probably known to most students. Guy agreed with their assessment, and they left his home with a feeling of partial success. It was abundantly clear that Sir Allard and Celeste had fallen foul of the Circle and both had met with disaster. Matthias did not feel inclined to meet with the girl again - they had the information they needed and Matthias was afraid it would endanger the girl if they did. The shame he had felt last night returned in the daylight. When in Italy he had used girls when the need arose, but all was done in fun and with intent... in his new life now there should be a restraint which he had not been able to control in that moment, and it disturbed him.

He found the streets crowded and dirty compared with the Italian towns he had travelled in previously. There was no peace to be had in this city and not all citizens were kindly disposed towards the English.

They left by the heavily fortified Porte St Denis, where they had entered, and crossed over the wide ditch outside the walls. The weather was still windy and rather chilly with an occasional glimpse of the sun.

Matthias reined his horse in as they reached the far side of the great ditch and looked back at the city. The gate through which they had come was a strong square building with two drawbridges. It had felt threateningly confining as they rode through under the watchful eye of a knight and two crossbow men. It had been built as a defence against the English in 1369 and English travellers were still regarded with suspicion and dislike by some. Old resentments lingered - that much was obvious as they had discovered....still picking off English soldiers one by one, using skilled girls from Paris.

At the edge of the ditch the water was shallower although filled with detritus. Something at the edge caught their eye. Slumped at the edge of the ditch and ignored by most travellers was the body of a young woman. She had been carelessly thrown down at the edge of the ditch like so much rubbish, her position caught by some rough vegetation.

The only reason they saw her was because Matthias had paused to look back, but as he leaned down his horse's neck for a closer look he could see that she had been beaten before her throat had been cut.

He had been about to call to the archers, but the sound died in his dry mouth as he recognised her. He knew her...had known her in the carnal sense the previous evening; she had paid dearly for giving him that information.

William looked at his white face, a sheen of sweat suddenly upon it.

"You know her, Matthias?"

"I do. It was she who gave me the answer we have sought."

"Then we must ride swiftly – have no doubt, Matthias. She has been tossed here as a warning to you, hoping you would see her. Let us put some distance between ourselves and this place."

Matthias knew he was right, but it disturbed him to dig his heels in and ride on, leaving the girl for someone else to discover – if indeed, anyone bothered. He was saddened to realise that he didn't even know her name.

It took three days of hard riding to reach Calais and Matthias couldn't help but look over his shoulder from time to time – afraid of repercussion. He remembered the tall elegant Frenchman and the shadow on the stairs. Monseigneur, whoever he was, must be controlling the subtle infiltration of the Calais camp.

He and William spoke little until they were safely aboard a cog bound for Poole. They had ridden fast and both were stiff and tired; other travellers joined them from time to time, but they had deliberately kept their hoods up and voices low when they needed to speak.

They avoided the Calais garrison, paid for their hired horses and boarded the cog with thankful hearts.

The weather for the crossing was not favourable and for once in his life Matthias was sea-sick. He crawled to the side of the deck and retched until there was nothing left. He felt utterly miserable – cold, wet through, empty – and somehow, dirty, too. He would so have preferred to stop at that St Denis Gate to draw attention to the girl - unwanted garbage, tossed in a ditch. Was it a warning to him? Keep out – this is what happens to girls who disobey- girls who step outside the

Circle. That was how the girl had described Celeste's behaviour – stepping outside the Circle.

Now, apparently, another one had stepped outside the Circle and had paid the same price – a price Allard had unwittingly paid, too.

The cog heaved its way through the Autumn sea, bucking frantically and threatening to cause Matthias more retching. He tried to concentrate on a home coming. He was alone on deck – William had taken himself to another place, rolled up in his cloak and was asleep, unaffected by the weather.

So who was the girl who had called on Sir Tobias? Presumably part of the Circle.....but why? Did the Circle need money or was this just a cruel, spiteful act? Why bother to move to England... it didn't make sense. Why not leave it all in France? He dozed uneasily, turning events over in his mind.....his brief encounter with the girl had been noticed...perhaps even observed....overheard.....the savage punishment inflicted on her for speaking to him ....the news he had to bring home that Sir Allard was dead....the private knowledge of his own unexpected need with the girl.....and his return, as he realised how dry his mouth was, which he hoped would bring him once again to a normal, peaceful, existence.

The October days shortened, and as they did so the patience of the Sherborne townspeople shortened with them. They felt oppressed by the Abbot's resilient attitude for he had not honoured his promise to the Bishop of Salisbury. There was no relenting of the restrictions placed on the Abbey and the townspeople were smarting under his strident attitude. Little contact was made by the monks who distributed alms, and the situation was becoming very tense.

Apprentices, and even their masters, were fuming under a veneer of civility which would not last long. To make matters worse, even the townspeople did not seem to be of one mind; there were numerous fallings out amongst the populace. Where there had been friendships, suddenly there was ill feeling, and the situation was becoming explosive which fuelled disputes and arguments between men and women who had been neighbours for years. The illegal font was still in place in All Hallows, and no attempt had been made to widen the doorway from the Abbey to the Chapel of Ease.

The butcher, Walter Gallor, was such a man as supported the Abbot's views. His relationship with the Abbey was very cordial....even more than cordial... he supplied such meat as the Abbey wanted, and had, so it was rumoured, ridden out with the Abbot's hunting party from time to time to hunt deer in the Bishop of Salisbury's forest.

He had collected a little coven of supporters round him, enticing them to agree with his view, which was that the Abbot should be supported in his jurisdictions, and respected for his good works.

"What good works?" jeered John Baret as he surveyed the mess left by the monks and their builders in the nave of the great church.

He had come, with his wife, to petition the work force to clear some of the rubble before they closed the work off for the Winter months.

They had erected a thatch covering over the Eastern bay of the new work, but there was still a great muddle of timbers, uncut stone and discarded tools. Rosana Baret looked at it and wrinkled her nose.

"If it stays like this all the Winter there will be some spoiled tools...how can they justify such mess in God's house?"

"I must speak with Richard Vowell," decided her husband. "He may have some sway with the Abbot, being one of his selected priests."

"I doubt it," rejoined his wife, "he has spoken very openly against the unremitting quarrel with Abbot Bradford and fallen out with him over his views."

"Richard Rochell and the others shall hear of this; it is time we had some decisive action," John decided, grimly.

He met, that very evening, with like minded friends in the parlour of The Julian hostelry.

"We need to decide what to do," declared William Hoddinote. He swirled the ale in his tankard angrily.

"Baptisms will still be in our own Chapel of Ease. We have the new font," said a defiant John Baret. His own first grandchild would be baptised within days.

"It's the rubble and spoilage left in the nave which concerns me greatly," mused another. He was himself a master craftsman, and waste of materials and careless handling of tools grieved him.

"Baptism of infants is the prerogative of the abbey," a strident voice broke in.

The men looked up. Walter Gallor was standing in the doorway, arms akimbo, his red face scowling at them. "This nonsense needs to be halted. We cannot have two fonts serving the same parish."

Richard Vowell rose, meeting Walter's heated, hostile eyes.

"So be it...Our good Bishop Neville decreed nearly a year ago that the processional arch should be widened.

When the Abbey sees fit to do their part, we shall do ours. Meanwhile, I intend to baptise infants there very shortly."

"Font first....doorway second." Walter spoke with gritted teeth. He was a big man with a determined temper, and he saw this declaration of forthcoming baptisms as a wicked insult to Mother church and the Abbot.

"A man like yourself should be supporting your fellowmen. This is hypocrisy so you can hunt the Bishop's deer with the Abbot. You cannot run with the deer and hunt with the hounds." The words were out of Henry's mouth before he could stop them.

Walter took a step forward, fist raised. John stood up in haste.

"Now Walter," he said, placatingly, "Let's not have trouble so publicly. Henry spoke without thinking."

"What if I didn't?" Henry taunted, his face mottled with drink. " The Bishop and the Abbot have us tied up well here in Sherborne – and you should be one of us, Walter Gallor, not siding with them...you and your friends.....look at you...what are you? Some side line of the Abbey? Ale is more expensive in Sherborne thanks to the Bishop's tax of Croukpenny, and the Abbot cares not one jot for our souls...nor for the poor of this town. He is a self important, self serving hypocrite..."

"Enough, Henry!" John Baret exclaimed, afraid the young man had gone too far.

"Drink talks, Henry," William Hoddinotte admonished. He glanced at Walter's huge frame and flushed face. He too, was well in his cups.

"You will regret that, Henry Goffe," Walter muttered, as he turned and left the house.

Mine host, Margaret Goffe, laid a hand on Henry's shoulder.

"You have said too much, son," she said quietly. "Walter is a hot character...it does not do to anger him. The issue of Croukpenny has nothing to do with this dispute with the Abbey...it is a tax imposed by the Bishop of Salisbury and we have become used to it, however unfair it appears to be. We just have to charge a little more for our ale."

"Turn to good events, mistress Goffe," interposed Richard Vowell.

"How is the fund for the poor house progressing?"

Mistress Goffe was pleased to be able to say that despite the ill feeling and quarrelsome nature of the town, people had been surprisingly generous in their donations. She herself had donated the Julienne as a property from which the almshouse would directly benefit, and several other noteworthy citizens had promised support for the scheme. It was a thing which was at variance with the current ill feeling regarding the font.

Talk turned to other matters, but Henry's words to Walter Gallor would have a terrible effect on things.

Chapter 8

Matthias was relieved to be home. He was exhausted, dirty and still experienced a sense of shame for passing the murdered girl on the St. Denis gate, and his dalliance with her which caused her downfall. Before making for his own home, he and William gave Sir Tobias their account of the expedition.

"So it would appear that Allard is indeed dead. Of that we are now certain. But what has become of this girl masquerading as Celeste? Celeste herself appears also to have paid a terrible price for their attachment."

It was obvious to Sir Tobias that Allard had deserted his daughter and young son, become hopelessly infatuated with Celeste, and the fact now needed to be faced.

"His infidelity cost him dear," William observed.

"But what of the situation in France?" Matthias asked, rubbing his weary eyes in frustration. His orderly mind liked to tie things up neatly, and this was still a tangle of loose ends.

"We may never understand it, Matthias," Sir Tobias said, "the camp in Calais is clearly in disarray. The men have not been paid for months. The death of John, duke of Bedford was a disaster for our troops in France. Duke Humphrey is being replaced by Duke Richard of Gloucester. This may improve matters. It is a matter of grave concern to England that our King is so young. We can only pray that he will come to manhood and prove to be as strong in government as was his father before him."

On this sombre note, the talk broke up and Matthias mounted his horse and made his way home to Milborne Port.

He reflected on the events which had unfolded in Paris as he rode. Allard and Celeste had met with an untimely and violent end; at least the uncertainty of Allard's fate was now clear and Alice was released from her marriage vows. No doubt Sir Tobias would be seeking a new match for her in the fullness of time. Matthias hoped the choice would be more secure than this one had been.

The state of the camp in Calais appeared to give Sir Tobias cause for concern for the country in general... Matthias respected his knowledge but had no first hand experience of battle. Of course, he was required to keep up his practice at the butts with his bow....as were all the men in the area, but it had become somewhat half hearted of late. He had been glad of William's presence while in France, and discomfited by the antagonism towards the English from some quarters. It was the mystery of the false Celeste which troubled him. He failed to understand why anyone would trouble to seek out Sir Tobias and Alice on a paltry excuse to extract money....it was not as if the events had happened in England....why pursue the family of one soldier who had been in Calais all the way to Dorset on a false premise? And where had this girl disappeared to?

Fresh doubts and concerns assailed him as his home came into view. He had been away longer than he had intended; how had Alice fared with his pupils? Had she been kind to Martin, who had brought her the original news of Allard's desertion....and had he lost any pupils through his time He tethered his horse quietly and entered through the back kitchen.

Elizabeth rose to her feet with an exclamation of pleasure.

"Master! We were beginning to feel troubled for your safety. Have you eaten? Where is your horse?"

Matthias hushed her gently.

"Let me listen to the sounds of the schoolroom before they know I am home," he replied.

He sat on Elizabeth's wooden settle and stretched out his legs, suddenly content to let the peace of his home wash over him.

He heard Alice's voice, reading aloud one of the stories he had advised her to use. He heard Martin's voice in the background, correcting a single boy's copying. He closed his eyes and allowed other sounds to invade his senses....Elizabeth was moving smoothly around the kitchen, stirring broth....the smell was fragrant and enticing.....rooks cawed from outside high in the trees, indignant and quarrelsome birds, Matthias thought, dreamily. A horse neighed and his own horse whickered in response...Davy had returned from some errand. His footsteps were brisk, and as he opened the door, Matthias realised how much he had been missed by his people. Davy's round face lit up with pleasure and relief, and Matthias experienced a feeling of belonging, and of the tranquillity of his home.

"Master! Welcome home! This is good news to have you back!"

"Has all been well here, Davy? I'm sorry it has been so long."

"We've all managed very well, but I'm sure we will all be glad to see you safely home."

"I'll go in and see them when Alice has completed what she is doing."

"She has done very well with them," Davy volunteered, "but I'll let you see that for yourself, Master. I'll go and see to the horses."

Matthias was pleased to see that Alice and Martin had achieved an orderly schoolroom atmosphere, and from accounts they gave, there had been no trouble or difficulty from the boys. The parents had looked a little askance to begin with but soon realised that Matthias was on some business for the Coroner, and that he had left the boys in capable hands.

Both Martin and Alice seemed to have benefited from the experience; Alice had colour in her cheeks and was proud of the work she had done. Martin likewise held his head a little higher, and had lost the defeated look in his eyes. His blind eye was less red and angry, and he frequently saw flashes of daylight now.

After Lady Alice and Luke had departed for their home, Matthias sat with Martin in the kitchen for a while.

"You're managing with the crutch pretty well now," Matthias observed.

"My balance seems better with wood of the right size," Martin explained. "I have fashioned several new crutches for myself whenever I see a suitable piece of wood."

"You have some skill with wood, Martin. Perhaps you might make use of this in the future?"

Martin was silent. Matthias glanced at him. Martin seemed to be struggling for words.

"You are wondering whether this information we have brought back releases you from here?" Matthias guessed.

"Something like that," was the reply

"What have you in mind to do...or where to go?" Matthias asked him gently

A shadow crossed Martin's face. "I had hoped there might be room for me to stay here..... but I can see that is not possible now you are home....If I may stay for a little longer, I will go to Sherborne to seek some form of work. There are ale houses there...I could work as a pot boy..."

"You have more to offer than that!" Matthias exclaimed

"I have to be realistic," Martin replied, "I am almost blind in one eye and my amputation renders me slow and clumsy, although with the salves and ointments given to me by Elizabeth, I improve daily."

The Lady Alice delivered Luke herself the next morning. She was more relaxed with Matthias than previously, although pale and quiet in manner.

"I thank you, Matthias, for the trouble you have taken to discover the truth of my husband's....demise." She faltered over her choice of words, but met his eyes as she spoke. "I would be grateful if you would consider that we need not discuss it any further. The subject is closed."

Matthias bowed his head in acknowledgment. He hoped she would never discover how he had obtained the knowledge.

"Tell me how you think I can help Martin to find a new life," Matthias asked her, hoping to divert her sadness.

"It is difficult to say," began Alice, frowning as she thought over the last weeks, "He is able to read, he has a pleasant manner with the scholars and he has been most helpful to Lydia in his spare time. Clearly he has some skill with wood – he has fashioned several small dolls for the little girl, and he has been ever courteous towards me. What avenue can we suggest?"

"I cannot turn him out, although he has indicated that he is willing to go. I fear for him if he tries to go alone into Sherborne or any other town. He is more vulnerable than he thinks. "

"I fear if he goes, he will end up begging," Alice ventured, "Although your Elizabeth has potioned him regularly, I detect some pain when he is fatigued."

"What manner of tasks has he performed for Lydia? Were they household tasks?"

"It seemed to be chiefly minor repairs to the fabric of her house. It gave him a purpose when I had no need of him. I hope that was alright?"

"Very much so," said Matthias, with a smile, "for it was she who first helped him when he was destitute and in despair."

"I would that someone would do the same for me," Alice spoke with sudden bitterness as she turned her palfrey to return home.

Matthias remained silent. His recent need for the nameless fair haired courtesan who had given him the information seared his memory and he found it impossible to respond to her.

He watched as she rode away from him.

Martin used the nag to journey to Sherborne the next day. He had tentatively talked with Davy concerning his plans, and decided that he would gain nothing by waiting at Milborne Port...with Matthias now back in his school, there was no need for him to be on hand in the schoolroom. He would travel into Sherborne and assess the hostelries and ale houses for himself. Matthias gave his blessing to the loan of the nag, and he left the house early in the morning.

It was late October, and there was a strong breeze as Martin jogged down Cold Harbour, leading to the Green, where work might be available. He was not hopeful of finding work at any of the better hostelries. The George was too grand for the likes of himself, so he continued down Cheap Street, intending to turn up Hound Street to seek out lesser ale houses.

As he approached the turning, there was a rush of feet from the bottom of Cheap Street with much fevered shouting and he could see a press of bodies struggling into the narrow opening of the Shambles. Curious, he abandoned Hound Street, and continued down Cheap Street, following the noise of shouting, which soon became fighting. He could see punches being thrown, red faced angry townspeople attacking each other with staves, street stalls overturned with trampled goods in the gutters accompanied by raucous shouting and dogs swirling round the mass of people, barking shrilly at the disarray.

Anxious lest he became involved in a street affray, he skirted round the Shambles and into Lodborne, from where, as he remained mounted, he could see angry crowds, shouting and pushing to enter the Abbey Church. He eased the nag a little nearer. He could hear shrill accusations of vandalism...someone had smashed the font in All Hallows Chapel of Ease.... The crowds became more volatile, and fearing for his own safety, given his damaged appearance and lack of mobility, he eased the nag round and turned for home, using the lower track to avoid becoming involved in what look to be an unpleasant occurrence.

While Martin was making for Milborne Port via a more circuitous route, the scene inside the Abbey was frenetic. Furious townspeople armed with staves and fists strove to reach Walter Gallor, who was still smashing with ferocious energy the illegal font in All Hallows.

"What do you think you are doing? How dare you…" Richard Vowell, current priest in charge of All Hallows, arrived, pushing through the fomented crowd….

"This is the stand we chose to make…how dare you destroy our protest."

He surveyed the destruction of the font, pieces splintered and jagged, dust from the hammer blasts covering the floor and Walter Gallor's triumphant face as he stood panting with exertion.

"The next baptism will be in its rightful place…in the Abbey where it should be…" Walter hissed, fairly spitting in Richard's face.

Young Henry Goffe threw himself at Walter with raised stave but Walter's clenched fist blackened his eye before he could bring the stave down on Walter's huge head.

Richard Vowell could scarcely speak coherently, so great was his anger…friends tried to restrain him as he spat venom and fury at the destruction of the font. Fights now broke out between opposing sides in the main body of the Abbey Church, the nave still littered with building rubbish. Unseemly scenes of violence shattered the October day, monks appeared from their devotions...and what had started as a violent protest now became nothing short of a riot.

The clatter of horses hooves increased the hellish scene....support had arrived unexpectedly from the Earl of Huntingdon and his men. They laid about Walter Gallor and his friends as they fled the scene, making the green sward outside the Abbey a veritable battlefield.

What happened next was unimaginable. The Earl's men had been en route from Dartington to London, and were ripe for action. They quickly seized the initiative for revenge....whipped the already blood lusty Richard Vowell into leading the rioters into the abbey where much damage was done, but not content with that, he climbed high up onto the roof of All Hallows, cheered on by his rioting parishioners who watched with horrified glee as he sent a final warning to the Abbot....a fire arrow, soaring into the sky above the Abbey.

It took flight a little way, faltered, and descended, fanned by the wind, straight into the thatch covering the building work.

There was no chance that it would not ignite. The thatch had been erected to protect the unfinished work from the coming Winter weather, so the thatch was dry and the fire took hold quickly.

The angry mob was stilled as suddenly as they had begun, and then as one, their collective fire instincts took over, but it was too late. The fire burned relentlessly, spreading to the West of the nave, taking with it the choir, the bell tower and even the bells.

It was a scene from hell itself. The flames licked higher, devouring wood and staining stone, sparks dancing above the greedy slivers of angry flame. The Abbot watched in helpless horror as the flames rose ever higher, the heat intense.

"They have to pay for this," he muttered to Prior William. "The Bishop shall hear of this desecration."

There was a crash as the brickwork of the bell tower crumbled, and a collective moan of despair from watching monks, beaten back by flames.

"Keep back!" Shouted a fire-fighter, as the flames roared angrily.

"Back! BACK!" came the repeated cry as the flames shot up the bell tower.

The fire soon reached the roof from which molten lead began to fall like globules of glistening rain and people fell away from inside, leaving the Abbey to burn.

Townspeople had gathered on the green outside the church, watching in guilty dismay as the fire raged on. Some feeble efforts were made to douse parts of the building with water, carried in by local firefighters, their faces blackened and weary, but this was a vain attempt.

Finally, with a deafening crash which reverberated through the very ground, the bells and bell frame fell some 75 feet, causing some of the watchers to fall to the ground, covering their ears to block out the sights and sounds.

Abbot Bradford was white with fury and distraught at the sight of the terrible destruction, but there was little he could do save to gather his monks around him and retreat from the fierce heat still emanating from the damaged Abbey.

The crowd who had gathered on the green watched the flames in silent desparation and awe; no-one had thought it would end this way. There were sure to be serious repercussions in the days to come.

There were indeed, but not quite what had been expected. The heat from the ruined stones was intense, and it was three days later before any person was able to approach the site; the foreman of the masons sifted through gingerly on day three, and was appalled to discover the charred and blackened form of a body, much shrivelled and disfigured, lying under some burnt out beams which had been used for scaffolding.

"Coroner needed," murmured Prior William, as he dispatched a messenger to Purse Caundle.

Sir Tobias surveyed the desolate scene from outside this once magnificent building, and reflected on the pride of the Abbot and the resulting anger of the townspeople. He guessed the Abbot would not let this disobedience go unpunished, despite his arrogance being the root cause of the unrest. He sighed as he handed the reins of his horse to a lad, and entered the place by the untouched great West door.

The smell of charred wood was thick in the air, and as he approached the site of the main fire, the unpleasant odour of charred flesh invaded his senses.

There was little chance of identification it seemed, for the clothes, if there had been any, were completely burned. The hair was singed and stubby as if the victim had tried to protect the head as the flames grew fiercer; the eye sockets were sightless. Some flesh had melted.. but the body had turned slightly on its side in a foetal position, and the part touching the ground had been somewhat protected by the stones underneath. Sir Tobias carefully knelt to see more closely. It was impossible to judge whether the figure had been alive or dead when the fire began; he could see no blood stain on the stones beneath the mangled form so he was surprised that no attempt had been made by the victim to escape the fierce fire. He could think of no-one who would willingly remain hidden in the face of such peril allowing themselves to be met with an untimely end under crashing, burning beams. Enough was left of the body to suspect that it was that of a woman.

Sir Tobias rose to his feet and indicated to a waiting monk that the remains should be moved and buried with due reverence.

Two lay workers belonging to the monastery came forward and as he watched, they carefully manoeuvred the poor corpse onto a board. As they did so, the bones crumbled pathetically under their touch, dislodging what was once a small gold ring, which had partly melted under the heat and in doing so had fused with the remaining flesh.

The molten fusing would have meant nothing to anyone but Sir Tobias; the hard gem stone in the centre of the ring had survived the furnace and he knew at once the identity of the corpse.

Chapter 9

"I have no doubt that the girl was killed unlawfully."

Sir Tobias and William were riding home to Purse Caundle together. The Coroner's troubled eyes raked the landscape as if to rid himself of the memory of his discovery. He recalled the Abbot's anger at the fire, his vehemence that the townspeople would pay heavily for their actions and his own realisation that this poor corpse was the woman who had called herself Celeste, which was nothing to do with the Abbot's problems, but which weighed heavily on himself.

William was silent. He had not seen the remains of the girl, but he had no doubt that Sir Tobias was correct – the bogus Celeste had met a most tragic death. Sir Tobias was vivid with his description. William was left with a graphic picture of the ruination of her flesh partly melted, her eyes sunken and glutinous, her hair, what was left of it, brittle, crumbling as the lay workers moved the corpse and the stench of burnt flesh. This was surely a death that no-one would wish on a fellow human being.

"I have no idea of her name, nor where she is from."

"Is that important?" William wondered. " If you are concerned about the report for the Sheriff, the facts are simple enough. It is your more personal knowledge which muddies the water."

"Personal knowledge is a dangerous thing, William. I try to be as honest and transparent as possible, but you are right – the knowledge I have should not make the report of her death difficult. It is the fact that this touches my family that leads me to stumble."

"Let me return to Sherborne tomorrow Sir Tobias, where I can make further enquiries. It would be useful to take Matthias, if he can free himself from his work. He has a useful head on his shoulders and he is aware of the delicacy of the situation. Furthermore, he has no family connections to concern him."

They found Matthias in the empty schoolroom, preparing quills and inks for the morning. It seemed an endless task, but Matthias liked to be prepared for his pupils well before they arrived. The Autumn day was drawing to a close, and the savoury smells of coney pottage coming from the kitchen reminded Sir Tobias that they must not linger too long lest the daylight fade altogether.

Sir Tobias admired the orderliness of the school room, looked at Luke's slate, fingered the crucifix hanging on the wall, stood for a moment contemplating the picture beneath the crucifix of Daniel in the lion's den before turning to Matthias, who was regarding him with a quizzical look. Sir Tobias was not conforming to type this afternoon. He waited for the Coroner to come to the point.

"Matthias - the firing of the Abbey in Sherborne – as you know the roof was fired by the townspeople and a great conflagration erupted. It has destroyed much of the new building as well as part of the choir stalls. That beautiful building is now in need of repair which will cost hugely. The Abbot is determined the townsfolk will pay for the damage." The Coroner sighed with frustration as he remembered the intransigence of the Abbot. He was also aware that he was putting off the main point.

"He cannot see that it is fruitless to continue to refuse to be the first to relent....such damage has been done, - not only to the structure but also to the relationships of the people of the town. I was called today by the Abbot to investigate and record a body found in the remains of the roof timbers of the Abbey." He paused, swallowing hard as he saw again the melted flesh, gelatinous eyes, scorched bone. He was finally reaching the purpose of the visit.

Matthias waited, alert. There was something more, he was sure. Sir Tobias did not usually come to tell him what he had been doing on a daily basis. He had heard news of the fire, indeed, who had not, but he had no cause to ride into Sherborne to see such a thing.

Sir Tobias took a heavy breath.

"I believe the body to have been that of the girl calling herself Celeste. She was burnt beyond recognition but under the charred bones was the remains of the ring Allard had given Celeste."

The thought that the girl was trapped there whilst the fire burned around her did not bear contemplation. The roar and crackle of the flames, the intense heat growing nearer and nearer, the first catching of her clothing as her terrified body tried desperately to free herself from however she was held, for he had no doubt that she was not there of her own choosing, or maybe she was? Might she have fallen and become unconscious? Sir Tobias tried to check his thoughts – he had experienced far worse than this. Was he getting too old, or was it because this whole matter had touched him personally?

Matthias's mouth dried, almost smelling the smoke, feeling the panic.

" Might she have been dead before the fire began?"

"It is possible. Nobody would have willingly remained in the Abbey once the fire began...and there was much noise and shouting prior to the fire, so I am told. If she had been conscious, she would have had time to run."

"Celeste's double is dead then," Matthias said, slowly, "and the real Celeste also."

The possible implication of this for Sir Tobias' family came into his head slowly.

"So... does this mark the end of the incident?"

He eyed the Coroner carefully. He had no doubt concerning the integrity of his friend, but he wanted to be sure. If it was simply the end of the strange affair, there would be no need to admit Sir Allard's desertion, no need to convey messages to Duke Humphrey warning him of the sly erosion of soldiers. Alice would simply become a widow due to war and the destruction of good men by clever courtesans would continue. There need be no stain, however slight, on the family of the Coroner.

Matthias waited no more than a heart beat

"Surely you have come to know me better than that, Matthias? I must send word to the sheriff that this death is an unlawful killing, and I must attempt to apprehend the perpetrator. It is also necessary to send messages to court to inform His Grace the King of the situation in the Calais camp, including the desertion of Sir Allard... anything less would be dishonest. I fear, however, that he will not have been the first to fall under the spell of these clever courtesans."

He exchanged glances with William, who understood only too well that the young King would not himself decide on any action; he had only recently been cajoled into governing, but relied heavily on advisors. Decisions would be taken by Lord Suffolk or Duke Humphrey most likely.

"The report will go to the Castle tomorrow for messengers to carry it to court, and the whole saga of Sir Allard's desertion and death need to be explained. Whether any action is taken is not my concern but Sir Allard's desertion must be noted. I cannot have him thought a hero in any way. However, I would still be pleased to understand why the girl and presumably her accomplice sought us out like this and more importantly, Matthias, to bring to justice whoever caused the girl to be in such a place with no means of escape. I suspect she may have been held there against her will. Is it too much to ask you to accompany William tomorrow to search for details in Sherborne? Somewhere there must be a clue to this poor girl's dreadful death. Alice and Martin could bear one more day in the schoolroom, if you are in agreement."

Matthias sighed inwardly, but outwardly he met Sir Tobias' troubled eyes. The Coroner was his friend, the matter touched him personally. Matthias could not refuse him.

"Of course," he replied, "Alice and Martin will enjoy another day in the school room, and it has certainly been good for Lady Alice."

He was afraid he had been too familiar and looked quickly at the Coroner to detect any disapproval but saw none.

"I'll bring Luke and Lady Alice over first thing tomorrow....be ready to ride off straight away, Matthias," William told him.

After they left, Matthias went out to the barn which had become Martin's temporary home. He knocked on the door and entered quietly. Martin was fashioning a wooden toy with his knife, gently smoothing it, positioning it in his hands before shaving extra pieces off to give it a better shape.

" Martin, are you able to help Lady Alice in the school room tomorrow?."

"Gladly, I enjoyed my time there." Martin's puzzled eyes sought Matthias for an explanation.

"A disturbing discovery in the Abbey needs further investigation. The girl who claimed to be Celeste has been found burned to death in the remains of the fire. Sir Tobias only recognized her because the body had the little gem stone remaining underneath the charred bones. The gold ring had melted and fused but the stone remained. It would seem that she had been deliberately trapped there and died...or .."

"Perhaps she was being punished for her failure to succeed with the claim for silver?" Martin finished, putting his knife down. He felt responsible for this whole business. He should have returned home to Shaftesbury without ever interfering in Sir Allard's business. It had brought nothing but trouble to this place, and this place had been so good to him. How could he repay them?

"I will be ready in the morning to do whatever Lady Alice requires," Martin said, giving the toy a final polish.

Matthias was cloaked and booted against the chilly early November weather when William arrived. October had fled in a flurry of morning mists and evening darkness, and now November promised morning frosts. The harvest had not been good this year, and people were afraid of the coming Winter. William was armed with his war belt; Matthias had his dagger in its sheath at his belt. Alice greeted him courteously, composed and looking more relaxed than she had of late. Martin hung back, anxious not to seem presumptuous in their presence. He couldn't help feeling that the death of the unknown girl was in some way his fault. If he hadn't appeared at the very moment of her leaving and had not seen her, she might still be alive. Matthias had tried to reassure him that whatever the outcome, she was obviously involved in something very dishonest, fraudulent and possibly treacherous.

William carried in his satchel the report from Sir Tobias to the Sheriff and also messages to Court regarding the affair in Paris, which he trusted would be taken by messenger from the Castle to the Duke. Before dropping down to Sherborne he and Matthias must call at the Castle first. The Constable of the Castle would be able to summon a suitable messenger. Sir Tobias felt that he had then done what was right.

Sherborne was a subdued town following the fire in the Abbey. The discovery of the body had not been widely known, but the consequences of the firing of the roof were troubling the townspeople who knew there would be repercussions. Abbot Bradford was demanding compensation for the damage, and his letters had already been dispatched to the Bishop of Salisbury. He would not rest until the townspeople had paid their due, and they were painfully aware of the cost to themselves. There was still considerable anger and dissension concerning the actions of Walter Gallor, the butcher who had smashed the font. He had supporters who believed the illegal font should never have been erected and who were vociferous in their opinions. On the other hand, the priest of All hallows, Richard Vowell, should not have allowed his passion to have spilled over to such an extent that he had fired the fatal arrow. No matter that he claimed he had not intended it to cause such devastation, the fact remained that it had been catastrophic. The townspeople awaited the punishment which would surely come when the Abbot and the Bishop had conferred. It did not bode well. There was a subdued and joyless atmosphere in the town, with much ill natured muttering.

After the rather austere visit to the Castle, the two men went first to the George Hostelry where they stabled their horses, and then walked down Cheap Street towards the Abbey. The work had stopped for the overwintering; the monks had cleansed as much of the debris as possible and there was really very little to see, but the two men felt that was where they should begin.

Matthias perched on a stone boulder, smelling the remains of the fire. It lingered in his nostrils unpleasantly, making him move restlessly as they deliberated a plan which might bear fruit. He was warmly dressed in a dark green woollen cotte-hardie over a quilted waistcoat, dark brown hose tucked into heeled leather riding boots. A woollen hat was pulled down well over his ears and he had thick leather riding gloves protecting his hands from the cold.

William wrapped his great cloak around himself as he suggested their only way forward was a walk through the town, lingering at shops and stalls, asking questions about possible strangers. It seemed an impossibly vague task Sir Tobias had set them, although in a small town, strangers were noticed and watched. Unfortunately, the unrest in the town had caused all attention to be directed at the happenings in the Abbey.

"Whoever we might be seeking has to eat," Matthias pondered, "so why not start with food stalls. He or she may have not had much coin, so the street stalls might yield some result."

There were street cries all round, together with urchins tugging at their clothes. William shooed them away and both men kept wary hands on their purses. Sherborne was no exception to poverty. The harvest had not been good this year - and there seemed more beggars than normal, or so William observed. He was more familiar with the town than Matthias.

They turned away from the Shambles where the fleshers worked and lingered at a stall selling hot pies. The aroma made Matthias' mouth water until he saw the seller's dirty hands grubbing around her uncovered pies. He shuddered and moved on, but William lingered. He understood the value of idle chatter.

"Good trade, mistress?" he asked, winking at her as he fumbled in his purse for coin. She simpered back at him, handling a pie with her grimy hands. Matthias noticed an open sore on one of her fingers. William took it from her, moving away from the heat of her brazier under the tray of pies.

"Where would I go to stay if I arrived in the town as a stranger and with little coin?" he asked her. She scratched at her vermin infested clothing as she considered his question. Matthias noticed that William had not yet bitten into the pie he was holding.

"Some would try the Golden Sun ale house sir, but there's also the Gooseberry. That's a cheaper place."

"Thank you, mistress, and good day to you!" William said, moving on. He still held the pie, now cooling rapidly, in his hand.

Matthias suddenly became fascinated by a beggar slouched on the corner of Lodbourne. He crouched down to him, trying not to be repelled by his smell, but attracted by his outstretched legs. The man looked up at him fearfully.

"Take care, Matthias," William whispered, "these beggars are not all they seem." Matthias studied the man. His eyes were half closed, ringed by purple shadows, his skin sallow and unhealthy; his broken teeth were blackened behind lips which were cracked and dry. His ragged sacking was held in place by a dirty rope belt, disintegrating with age and wear. What interested Matthias was his stump of a leg, onto which was fastened a rough wooden slat.

"Are you able to walk on that?" Matthias asked him.

The beggar licked his dry lips and tried to sit up straighter.

"Yes sir. A barber surgeon fashioned it for me and designed the attachments himself."

"Does it hurt?"

"Sometimes it is sore... I try not to take it off for fear of losing it. It is my life blood now."

"How long have you had it?"

"Two Summers, sir. I'm afeared it will wear out soon."

"May I look more closely?"

Behind him William bent to look more closely too, and at the same time thrust the still warm pie into the man's hand.

"Thankee sir." Before the simple words were out of his mouth he had taken a bite, juices running down his chin. He crammed the pastry encased meat pie into his mouth as if afraid of it disappearing.

Matthias took the opportunity to examine the crude slat, fastened to the man's knee with leather straps, which were now wearing thin. The straps were positioned above his knee and were tight, making his skin marked and sore.

"I thank you for allowing me to look," Matthias said. He took a silver coin from his purse. "You need new straps. Buy some new ones for yourself before these wear out."

The man's eyes filled with tears. He wiped his chin on the back of a claw like hand.

"How are you called?" William asked him.

"Raul the lame."

"Well, Raul the lame, I shall look for you the next time I am in Sherborne to buy you a second helping of pie. I think you have given my young friend here an idea which may benefit a friend of ours with an amputated limb."

"Which way to the Gooseberry Ale house?" Matthias queried.

Raul's face filled with concern.

"What business do you have there? There are better places for you to drink."

"No matter. If we dislike it we shall move on with haste," Matthias assured him.

"Go behind the Abbey, sirs....turn left and the Gooseberry is at the end. Beware of the House of Fair Maids nearby...although they will be asleep now. They work at night." He winked, knowingly.

"This sounds a promising place to begin," Matthias said, as they left Raul.

The Gooseberry was indeed a poor looking establishment.

The track had become muddy and uneven. The bush hanging over the door proclaimed it to be open for ale, but the door was hanging at an angle, a slattern lounged against the wall and scarcely moved to allow the two men inside. William ordered two pots of ale under the suspicious eyes of the inhabitants. A tinker and his flea bitten dog occupied one corner, his tray of wares on the earth floor beside him. A large part of the room was taken up by a group of poorly dressed, quarrelsome individuals who all seemed more concerned with shouting their ill conceived opinions at each other without listening to anyone. The noise from this group prevented William and Matthias from having any conversation at all.

Matthias studied them as he sank his nose in the pot of ale – not particularly good ale either, weak and without flavour. From the little he could make out they were all men from around these parts who had been stood down from their work locally due to the poor harvest. They were indignant, anxious and ill at ease at the presence of Matthias and William, strangers to them who might be spying on them for some reason. The general sense of unease which pervaded the town had spread even to these poor specimens.

After a short while William stood up to leave, and Matthias followed suit. As they left, William asked the slattern, still draped against the wall in an unlovely pose, whether there were any chambers above for travellers.

"Yes sir, but all empty until the next great fair. We don't do much business of that sort."

"Nothing doing there," Matthias said as they retreated down the track with some relief. He thought fleetingly of Martin's idea of finding work in the lesser ale houses. He could not equate Martin with a place such as The Gooseberry.

The Golden Sun was their next destination. Off a small sunless runnel leading towards the Abbot's fishponds, there was little golden about the place, neither was there any suggestion of sun, but it looked cleaner and slightly more welcoming than the Gooseberry.

"Time to try their food, I think," Matthias decided as they squeezed into a small table next to a stained beam.

A more than buxom serving wench appeared, torn cap at a rakish angle on her tangled curls which were escaping round her moon like face, eyes greedily consuming the two men for wealth.

"Sirs?"

"Some of your eel pie..if it's fresh...and two flagons of ale."

" Very fresh, sirs.... and well flavoured."

"And your rooms? Are they for hire?"

"Not at present, sir...they are taken and crammed full. We only have two and one of them is taken by a man who has paid double to have it to himself."

"Too much idle chatter!" A coarse male voice interrupted. Matthias turned to see Mine Host appear from the back of the establishment, a large man, running to fat, with a florid, sweaty face, and eyes squinting from under reddened puffy eyelids. His hands were like large hams, podgy fingers pointing accusingly at the wench.

She bobbed ingratiatingly and scurried off to fetch the pie.

"You want rooms?" he growled. "I can turn some out if you pay well."

"We'll see what the pie is like first," William told him. He retreated with a sneer of disbelief.

The pie was tolerable, even tender, and the ale was more acceptable than that of the Gooseberry.

"This man who has paid double, I wonder why?" Matthias pondered. William mopped the trencher with his horn spoon as he swallowed the last of the pie.

"We need to find the girl again. I warrant we'll get nothing from Mine Host – not because he has anything to hide, but just because He's the type who wouldn't give a dying man a swallow of water. I've met them before."

Matthias smiled wryly. He had thought much the same of the man.

However, the girl did not appear again and they were unwilling to engage the Host in further conversation.

They prepared to leave, feeling disappointed at their lack of progress. Both men got to their feet, but as they did so, a swarthy faced fellow slouched in, lurched to the table nearest them and called loudly for attention. Matthias and William sat down again, the better to observe. The fellow did not look well kempt; his long greasy hair was pulled back in a straggly queue, his tunic was spattered with mud and food stains, and his hose was snagged and pushed into well worn boots. Matthias noticed his hands were scratched in several places, dried blood mixed with grass stains. His face was thin and angular, the lips thin, his eyes angry.

"Ale..and quickly!" he snarled at the girl, who had now appeared again.

William caught Matthias' eye and they settled back on the bench in quiet conversation, waiting for any opportunity to approach.

"Bring hot water to my room," he ordered harshly, as she set the pot of ale in front of him.

"You are hurt, sir?" queried William, leaning over towards the fellow.

"Mind your business," was the curt response, as he picked up the ale and disappeared into the rear of the inn, where there were stairs which led to the sleeping chambers.

"A fine example of a man," William observed, with deep sarcasm, as they finally left.

"Is he worth following?" Matthias wondered.

"Nothing else so far has come our way," William agreed, "but it is flimsy – just because he has a surly manner and scratched hands...something had angered him, though."

The two men walked back up Cheap Street, passing the corner where they had first met Raul the lame. He was sprawled against the wall, sleeping. Matthias took the opportunity to look at the slatted wood fastened to him, and bought a sugared comfit which he put in Raul's outstretched hand. Raul didn't move, but Matthias hoped he would find it when he woke.

With no further leads, they reclaimed their mounts, and began the journey home.

Chapter 10

The child first heard the hooves as she lay down on the cold earth by the brook to drink. Terrified, she panicked and ran the wrong way, blundering through cruel brambles and catching her bare arms on ungainly twigs. She threw herself down, burrowing under the brush wood before forcing herself to lie still. Her breath was uneven and jagged, tearing at her thirsty throat. She needed to cough and clear the dust from her mouth; she tried to breathe more steadily to prevent the cough from coming. Her legs and arms were now bleeding slightly from the undergrowth where she had hidden.. ..but he mustn't find her...he mustn't. She had been so cold last night after she had fled from him, and so frightened, but she had escaped his clutches somehow. She knew it had made him angry; she had heard him shouting and beating at the plants and bushes around the hostelry. Fortunately he had been too drunk to follow her, but his last words hung in her head.

"I'll find you in the morning, you little bitch. Just like your mother, but you won't evade me after a night out in the cold."

The door had slammed and she had scrambled into an empty barrel outside the Inn and shivered there until first light before putting as much distance between the town and herself as possible. She had no idea of direction; in her terror she simply needed flight, and the ability to hide if she heard him pursuing.

Now she was certain her time was up. The hooves were steadily growing nearer, but there was no shouting...no beating of the undergrowth on each side of the track. She held her breath. The sound of the hooves slowed.

"This is where I thought I saw something," she heard a male voice say.

"It might be worth a look," another voice responded.

The child lay frozen, hardly daring to breathe. Her bare feet were blue with cold; she was dressed only in her night shift, now torn and muddy, for that was what she was wearing when he had approached her, leering at her as he lifted his tunic and made his move on her.

She heard the sound of boots pushing aside the bracken and bramble; a little moan of terror escaped her. She tried to push her hand into her mouth to prevent another sound.

"I heard something, William," she heard one of the men say. She tried to push herself into a sitting position to defend herself, but her nightshift was caught firmly on the wicked spikes of gorse. She had made noise by striving to move. The boots were coming nearer. In her panic, she was not as well hidden as she had thought.

Suddenly they were there, two men, standing one either side of her looking down at her. She strove to control her bladder. She would not disgrace herself in front of two unknown men.

"A child!" the younger one exclaimed.

"Who are you hiding from, my maid?" asked the older man.

"You must be frozen," the younger one said, bending to touch her skin. She shrank away from him, fear catching her.

CHAPTER 10

"Leave me alone! Don't touch me!"

"We wish you no harm, little maid," the one called William told her, gently. "We would help you. Someone has used you harshly. You cannot stay here without warm clothes and food."

The younger man took off his cloak.

"Let me wrap you in this. Ride on my horse with me and we will find you a safe place to rest."

She was deeply suspicious of these men. Where had they come from? Where were they going? Was she going to be taken back to the place from which she had fled?

He held his cloak out to her. She made no attempt to take it from him, trying instead to pull her night shift down to cover more of her body.

"We are going home," William told her. She had no idea where that was, nor which direction...if she could even remember from which direction she had come.

Suddenly easy tears overtook her. Matthias, for that was his name she had learned, crouched down to her, squatting in the brambles.

"My house is where we are going," he said. "We are not going into the town."

"Please don't find the man again.." she sobbed "my mother ran away...and she didn't come back...."

Over her head, William and Matthias exchanged uneasy glances.

"Come, my maid, let's get you out of these prickly brambles and wrapped up warmly."

She offered no more resistance. She was frightened, exhausted, frozen and starving. Matthias wrapped his cloak around her thin form and lifted her gently onto his horse, mounting behind her. He took the reins.

"Hold on to the saddle horn," he told her, as they moved off.

He could feel her trembling inside his cloak as they rode, whilst he and William discussed quietly what they should do, where they should take her.

"If the man is the same one we encountered in the Golden Sun, then I think our day may have been well spent," Matthias murmured softly.

"It sounds as if he was up to no good with this child. He is clearly not her father. She mentioned her mother. Could it be that this is what we have been seeking?"

They were but half an hour away from Barton Holding and Matthias was glad to relinquish the burden of the child from his saddle when they arrived. She hadn't stopped trembling all the way, whether from fear, cold or uncertainty about her horseback ride Matthias couldn't tell, but it meant he had to concentrate very hard on keeping the frail child steady in front of him.

Elizabeth helped the little girl down from Matthias' horse carefully, perturbed at her appearance and her uncontrolled shivering and took her into the kitchen.

In a daze, the child let herself be washed, her cuts and grazes tended, and her night shift removed. Elizabeth wrapped her in a rough blanket and prepared some broth but she was too tired to feed herself, and it was Lady Alice, coming in to the kitchen with an apologetic knock, who sat by the child and coaxed her to eat a little.

"I think my father should know of this," she said to Matthias, who came in to see how the strange child was faring.

"I don't believe she knows where she is," Matthias offered, "she had no idea of direction – only that she didn't want to be anywhere near the man. She can't be more than six or seven Summers old."

"The man?" Alice queried, thoughtfully, "Matthias, leave me with the child a little. Perhaps I can coax the story from her."

Elizabeth busied herself with chores quietly near the window, leaving Alice space to talk with the child.

"What are you called?" she asked softly.

There was no answer. The child fluttered her eyes warily, uncertain of her safety.

"My name is Alice. I live near here. I have a little boy called Luke."

The child turned her head away from Alice as if she didn't want to hear this.

"Were you out all night? That was a very brave thing to do."

Still no answer.

"I expect it was very cold. Did you have anything to eat?"

The child shook her head.

"What happened to your clothes?"

" He took them."

A beginning, at least.

"Who is he?"

No answer. The child's lip trembled.

"A friend of your mother's?"

A nod of the head

"What is your mother called?"

"She ran away." A tear fell.

Alice trod carefully.

"Why?"

"He beat her....he pulled her hair....he fought on top of her on the floor."

Alice suddenly understood what the child had witnessed.

"What happened then?"

"My mother ran away from him. He chased her but he fell down at the door when she hit him...she didn't come back. She told me to run but I didn't run fast enough...he caught me..." suddenly the words came tumbling out.

Alice recounted the story as she understood it to Matthias when the child had worn herself out with talking and fallen asleep, still wrapped in the blanket.

"I'm not quite sure why they were there, but they were originally in a different place...I can't make out why they moved to the Inn. They seem to have had some business in the area...the Mother had to dress up and go out with him and then he got very angry...Matthias, it almost sounds as if her mother could have been the girl who called on us. Do you think that's a very fanciful notion?"

"It seems possible," Matthias conceded. "We encountered an ill tempered man at the second inn we visited. We planned to return tomorrow to talk further with him. He had blood stained hands..not hugely, but enough to possibly have searched rough ground for the little maid."

"Did you speak with him?"

"We tried, but he flung away from us and retreated further into the inn... it was a poor place, although not as wretched as the first one we tried."

"The child will need clothes, Matthias. She cannot stay wrapped in a blanket all the time...and we have to decide how to proceed."

He noticed the 'we' with unexpected warmth. He had not been able to speak so unreservedly with Lady

Alice before, except when speaking of her work in the school.

"He intended to violate the child," her tone was shocked and angry.

"It happens, Lady Alice.

"Alice will be sufficient.....I am just Alice." She had not intended to sound so flat, but her lack of self worth burst from her unexpectedly.

Matthias deliberately ignored her bitter statement. He had uncomfortable thoughts of his own, one of which was that this was the third girl he had met whose name he did not know. The first was the bogus Celeste, the second was his informant in Paris, and now this child, who may be giving them the answers they sought. At least he was aware of Alice's name. However much he wanted to dwell on Alice, he could not rid himself of the knowledge of the price the unknown girl had paid for his urgent need for her....and the payment had been intended for information, not for her services. Perhaps she had been killed because he was English... or maybe it was to prevent any more girls betraying The Circle...whatever the reason, it weighed heavily on him....a weight he could barely understand himself, when he considered the nights in Italy, when he and a few companions would seek out the best bordellos in carefree mood.

Alice and Elizabeth began deliberating quietly how to clothe the child on the morrow. Luke was four and a boy, and his garments were in Purse Caundle. Nothing of Elizabeth's would be suitable. She might well have to make do with her night shift, which Elizabeth could wash and mend, and a blanket to cover her.

Lost in his own dark thoughts, Matthias came to a sudden, unexpected decision which startled even himself.

"There is a chest in the solar. It contains some clothes which belonged to my sisters. I have not been minded to look at them. Mother used to keep some garments she particularly liked as we all grew up....Elizabeth, show Lady Alice where they are. I would prefer not to choose, but there may well be something there which would fit the child."

Without a word, Elizabeth ushered Lady Alice through the schoolroom and into Matthias' own room, from where they were able to mount the ladder towards the solar and sleeping chambers above. Matthias sat by the sleeping child in the kitchen, knuckles clenched. He had not thought to open the chest and bring back memories of his dead family.

He held his head in his hands as the past flooded back. He could hear his sisters' rich laughter, see their fair hair escaping from under their caps as they raced through the meadow, remembered the way their skirts whisked in the flurry of running away from him as he chased them with a pig's bladder filled with water. He must have been about fourteen and almost ready to leave for Oxford...they had collapsed in the barn, shouting to their father for help as Matthias had sprayed them....and then much later, on his frantic return years later, the silence of the house after the funerals. He had allowed Martin to make his temporary home in that same barn. Now perhaps he was a step further on his way, allowing the opening of his mother's chest.

Lady Alice and Elizabeth returned with several garments. Matthias did not look at them; Alice would have spread them out for him to see, but Elizabeth's warning look stopped her and she realised there were unshed tears in Matthias' eyes.

"Let the child sleep," Elizabeth suggested, to allow her Master time to recover. "I will dress her in the morning."

Lady Alice rose to leave. It seemed time to allow Matthias some privacy. "I will ask Father to come early tomorrow. He will know what to do." She glanced at Matthias. He brushed the tears from his eyes and stood up.

"Thank you both for your help. We may be some way to finding answers to this odd tale."

William and Lady Alice rode away with Luke trotting between them, and Matthias returned to the school room to hear from Martin how the day went.

"It seems I have developed a taste for collecting waifs and strays," Matthias ruefully acknowledged.

Martin tried to smile at what he knew was a harmless remark, but he felt belittled at being described as a stray.

"The little girl may be able to help us, Martin. There were two places they stayed in, and she seems to think her mother has disappeared. We need to look at this story in more detail in the morning."

"Are you thinking her mother could have been the girl calling herself Celeste?" Martin asked. Matthias nodded thoughtfully.

"It could be, but why would she have been travelling with a child?"

"There were no children in the Calais camp. The girls came on their own. It was no place for children."

"Maybe it is a false idea, but there is certainly some value in pursuing it. The finding of the child was a stroke of good fortune. Poor little thing; she was terrified and extremely cold. I fear if we had not found her she would have died of cold before morning."

The two men fell silent as they both imagined the cold seeping into the small body, and the chance of anyone finding her frozen body, half hidden as it would have been by brambles.

"I almost forgot to tell you about a beggar we saw in Sherborne," Matthias exclaimed, changing the subject abruptly.

He was excited as he told Martin the details of the beggar Raul, and suggested to Martin that they should look for some suitable wood to fashion a similar aid.

"I have seen something like it in France," Martin admitted. "I had not thought to fashion the same for myself....I am unsure how to fix it or whether it would rub too much or be harmful to the wound."

"We need the advice of a physician," Matthias opined.

Martin smiled sadly. He spoke with resignation.

"Master Barton, I am a simple man. I do not have good silver to pay a physician. I do not have work; I am not resident in any one place. As you yourself said, I am nothing but a stray."

Matthias felt the colour rise in his face as he realised that his thoughtless remark had caused distress. He must have sounded patronising to Martin.

"I did not mean to cause you hurt, Martin. It was a careless word spoken without feeling. Forgive me."

The two men parted in an agreeable silence as the light faded to give way to a November evening.

Chapter 11

Sir Tobias was keenly interested in the happenings of the day. William had outlined the main points, and he arrived at Barton Holding in the morning, delivering Luke for his schooling himself.

With Lady Alice not present, Matthias needed to be with his scholars until he had set them some copying which he could ask Martin to supervise.

Elizabeth had helped the child to dress in the clothes Lady Alice had found in Matthias' chest. Matthias steeled himself to see his sisters' garments on another child, but they were not the clothes he remembered very clearly....his mother had put away certain favourite robes and tunics from early childhood, and his sisters had been eleven and thirteen when they were taken by the sickness.

Elizabeth had done her best with the child. She was clean and tidy and had timidly eaten some bread and honey. She had spoken very little apart from disclosing her name – Ennis.

Sir Tobias met her in Elizabeth's kitchen, where she felt most secure.

"Sir Tobias is a good man," she told Ennis before he came in, treading softly. "He will help you. Just talk to him."

Ennis pressed her lips together. She would not say anything which would allow anyone to take her back to the man.

Sir Tobias found Ennis surprisingly uncommunicative and was relieved when Matthias managed to join them.

"Hello, Ennis! You look better this morning. How are your hands?" Matthias began, cheerfully.

Ennis held them up. The scratches were still visible, but were drying up well. She looked at him with relief; Matthias she recognized, but Sir Tobias seemed too important for her to speak to.

"Where do you live when you are with your mother?" Matthias asked her gently.

"A long way away." Ennis whispered, looking at Matthias only. She remembered she had felt safe on his horse. Maybe she could trust him.

"Over the sea?" Matthias asked.

Ennis smiled a little. "Oh no, we came here in a big cart. My mother was happy because she had found work."

"With the man?"

Ennis shivered. She nodded.

"My mother is very pretty," she volunteered, speaking directly to Matthias.

"Does she have fair hair, like yours?"

Ennis nodded again.

"The man was very angry that she had brought me with her, but I couldn't stay alone. When my mother went out working with him I had to stay behind."

"When did she work with him?" Sir Tobias asked.

Ennis looked at him, but now she had spoken with Matthias, she seemed more confident, and she put her head on one side as if considering.

"Quite a lot of days ago," she said, slowly. "Then suddenly he was horrid...I saw him beat her...he hit her hard...she ran away but he caught her by the hair and dragged her back..." she stopped, tears coursing down her cheeks.

Lady Alice had told them that what Ennis had described sounded as though the child had witnessed a rape as well as a beating, and thankfully had not understood what she was seeing. There was no need to make Ennis re-live that.

Sir Tobias held out his hand and disclosed the burnt gem stone from Sir Allard's ring.

"Do you remember seeing this with your mother?" he asked.

"The man gave it to her. He made her wear it when she went out one day to work, but it was on a ring.... not just the pretty stone." She looked puzzled. "Where is my mother? What happened to the ring?"

Sir Tobias exchanged glances with Matthias, who shook his head slightly.

"Will you stay here with Master Barton and his people? You will be safe here while I ride to Sherborne to talk to him."

A look of pure fear crossed Ennis' face. "You won't bring the man here, will you," she whimpered., suddenly very much the terrified child again.

"No. Elizabeth will look after you," Matthias assured her.

He returned to the schoolroom with a heavy heart. Life was becoming so complicated. Sir Tobias had conferred with him before he had ridden off with William to Sherborne to accost the man. Ennis' story had given them a much needed lead, but it was far from clear. How was this connected to Calais? Was Calais just a red herring? All it had achieved was to verify the death of Sir Allard, although that had been necessary. How had Allard become tangled up in this? And what was to become of Ennis? If her mother was indeed the burned corpse in the Abbey, then she needed shelter, comfort and a place to call home. He knew he was not able to offer that.

Sir Tobias called first at the Castle to talk with the custodian. He was deeply suspicious of the man Ennis had described, and who it appeared Matthias and William had encountered briefly. There were still a handful of soldiers lodged at the Castle, men of the Earl of Huntingdon's company, remaining there on guard, although there was little to guard in the normally peaceful market town. However, the unrest in the town had caused some very real concern. Knives had been drawn, brawls had taken place, the rioting in the Abbey had been an unpleasant, ugly scene. The Earl of Huntingdon had seen fit to leave a small party of men at the castle to attempt to control rising tempers in the town. The butcher, Walter Gallor, had gone to ground; his shop was shut for, although he couldn't afford to lose business, neither could he afford to lose his life. He decided to lie low until tempers cooled. He had supporters, but they had been less vociferous, at least for the moment.

William led Sir Tobias to the Golden Sun hostelry. It was shabby but clean, rushes on the floor were no more than a day old. There were several old men slouching on upturned barrels enjoying ale, their talk only of the riots in the Abbey, the Abbot's demands for compensation and how things had been better when they were young. Younger men were not in evidence...no work would mean no pay, and few could afford that.

Sir Tobias called for the Inn keeper. He appeared, smiling ingratiatingly when he recognized the Coroner.

"My best ale for you, Sir?" he oozed.

"Thank you...not this morning. Tell me, what customers do you have overnight at present?"

The inn keeper's face fell. He would like to have described the Coroner as a customer.

"Several, my lord Coroner. Might you be interested in someone particularly?" He held a greasy hand out hopefully. Sir Tobias ignored it.

"A fellow who had a young child with him...."

" He left at first light. When you find him, bring him back...he left without settling his bill," was the angry reply. "The child appears to have gone missing. He was trouble. A stranger, and rough with the child. He spent a long time looking for her yesterday, and came home without her."

Sir Tobias laid a coin on the counter for the information; the inn keeper took it greedily.

"Would you like to see the room, Sir?"

"Have you checked it?" Sir Tobias asked him, anxious to waste no time in finding the stranger.

"I have, Sir. He left nothing."

"Then we'll not look ourselves. But should he return, unlikely I suspect, send word to the Castle."

As they turned to go one of the old men caught William's arm.

"He was a soldier. He had calloused fingers and strong arms and the marks of a wrist guard. I reckon he had been a bowman."

"He was in a fair temper when he came in last night..." another volunteered.

Sir Tobias called to Mine Host..

"Give these valiant observers some more ale, inn keeper." He tossed some coins on the table for them.

They spent most of the day checking hostelries, out-buildings and asking after strangers who had been seen with a child and possibly a fair haired woman. It was late in the day as they were returning to collect their horses when they finally had some useful information.

The horses had been stabled at the George Inn which had a small barn to one side for storage of hay. William looked in at the door of the barn as Sir Tobias unhitched their mounts. He noticed in one corner there was a small mound of hay which had been fashioned to form a nest, large enough for a person. He called the stable boy to him. There was no secret...the boy readily told him that there had been a man with a lady and a young child sleeping in there for two nights some three or four days ago. They had left and he had not raked the hay back into the main pile in case they returned. He had been given a few coins for his trouble.

No, he said, the man had not returned alone, he was sure because he slept himself in a far part of the barn and he would have heard him.

Sir Tobias recalled that the bogus Celeste had looked unkempt and tousled on her second visit, as if she had slept rough. He was sure they were now on to the right trail.

Chapter 12

Matthias met with Sir Tobias and William to review what they had learned. They met in Purse Caundle where Sir Tobias' scribe had laid out inks and parchments at Sir Tobias' request.

"Martin Cooper arrived at Purse Caundle in July with news of Allard's desertion," he began. The quill scratched energetically as Thomas conveyed the words.

"He returned later in the Summer hoping for help and shortly after that, the girl calling herself Celeste visited me." He tapped his fingers on the table, recalling the events.

"Martin saw the girl the following day on her return visit and denounced her claims."

"I don't think we have any doubts now concerning Martin's honesty in the matter," Matthias ventured, interrupting the flow.

"I would agree," the Coroner commented. He glanced at Thomas, who had paused to sharpen his quill.

He continued when Thomas was ready, "The girl disappeared and could not be traced, but confirmation of Allard's wherabouts needed to be established. Matthias and William travelled to Calais to ascertain the facts,"

Matthias remembered the hostility of the streets in Paris, the fear felt by Guy's wife and the body of the courtesan by the city gate.

"We seem to have achieved one thing. We have learned without doubt that Allard is dead, together with the courtesan Celeste. We have also realised that there is a slow but deadly organized movement to pick off English soldiers in the Calais camp using a group of girls, of whom Celeste was one. The information has been conveyed to His Grace the King."

"It is at this point that the water tends to be a little muddy," Matthias said, frowning as he tried to organize the events into a chronological order.

"It occurs to me that the Calais camp is possibly irrelevant to us now," Sir Tobias mused. "The child is clearly associated with the bogus Celeste, and she was quite adamant that their journey did not involve a sea journey."

"So what are your thoughts?" William queried. He had been silent, listening intently to the catalogue of events.

"The couple who are seeking money from me are fraudulent. That much is obvious, but why they have not targeted Allard's father, I cannot think."

"Possibly they are unaware of his father's existence, or maybe they had intended to move onto him and extract further coin," Matthias said, "but the fire in the Abbey and the unrest in the town has played into their hands, or should we say into his hands. Perhaps the girl was not as committed as he?"

"She was certainly quite vicious to Martin when he denied her story," Sir Tobias remembered.

"At that point I'm certain she was very much part of the game," Matthias said. He recalled the spiteful words regarding Martin, and how her face had changed to rage, fairly spitting out her coarse accusations against him.

"So," continued Sir Tobias, "a further Item: they remain in the area to rethink their strategy; their presence is largely unnoticed because of unrest in the town."

"Yes, - I did find it strange that no-one had taken note of strangers. In a small town, strangers are normally noticed and talked about. People want to know where they are from, and more importantly, why they have come, but nobody seemed to have noticed them."

"The stable boy was very vague about how long the barn had been used. Maybe they stayed there longer than he remembered, and folk have been very wrapped up in the confrontations in the Abbey. They certainly used a hostelry for a few days; they were remembered there."

"Well, the man was remembered," Matthias corrected William, "The Golden Sun only mentioned the fellow. There was no mention of the girl."

"That was after the fire in the Abbey; if we are right, she would have been dead by then."

It was a thought that sobered the discussion.

"We need to search for this fellow. He may have killed the woman. If not, he certainly caused her death, and he clearly intended to use the child for other less savoury purposes."

"I will call on the Castle for help in the morning," Sir Tobias decided. "We need to do a comprehensive sweep of the town and find this man."

As Matthias rode home, he contemplated the fate of the child. Where was she to go? Sir Tobias had not mentioned her at all, presumably because he had other more personal implications in this affair. Lady Alice appeared calmer and more accepting of events, but the facts were that she was now widowed, her whole life in front of her still, the stain of her husband's desertion lying heavy on her. He would need to find her a suitable match, not now an easy task with a child from the first husband. She had been the wife of a knight, the daughter of a knight...how would she fare now? Despite his unacknowledged feelings towards her, he knew she was out of his reach.

The November night was chilly, with the promise of a first frost. Dead leaves carpeted the ground in places, bare twigs scraped together as an Autumn wind tickled the stillness of Barton Holding. A moonless night yielded an air of unusual tension about the house.

Martin had spent the early part of the evening in the kitchen with Davy and Elizabeth. He had considered the idea Matthias had mentioned; Davy had found him a piece of wood which he sat and looked at for a long time before taking up his knife. He stared at his stump, memorising the shape of it. If he was going to wear this wood, it would need to be fashioned very exactly to mould round what remained of his limb. Ennis had watched when he started work, fascinated by the slowness, the gentleness of his movements. He needed it to be hollowed out at the top to fit round what remained of the leg. It would need to be smooth, and to have grooves around the top to hold the straps Matthias had described. It would not be an easy thing to make, but he was a patient worker, and he could try again if his first effort was unsuccessful.

For the moment, Matthias had requested that Elizabeth have charge of the child whilst it was determined what should be done. She was safe here, and appeared less nervous of them all. She had without doubt provided the key to finally moving forward.

Now he was ready to retire to his place in the out-building which he had made comfortable for himself. Regretfully he knew he must move on. Matthias had paid him for his work in the schoolroom; Martin had been reluctant to take the coins, but Matthias had insisted, so he was in receipt of a little coin. He lowered himself onto his bed and stretched out, listening without fear to the night sounds. It was owls which he could hear tonight, floating on their outstretched wings over the meadows, hunting for prey like so many grey ghosts.

He remembered the night sounds he had heard when he slept uneasily outside Lydia's cottage, every rustle threatening his safety. He thought of Lydia with a little warmth. He had been pleased to do some small tasks for her, and she was easy with him, ignoring his wretched condition. He would miss her. He was so much more confident now. So much had happened to him since he had first stumbled towards the home of the Coroner. He had found unexpected kindness and understanding from the Coroner himself, the friendship of Davy and Elizabeth and the respect of Master Barton and Lady Alice. Sleep began to drift over him pleasantly.

The furtive scratching at the door did not disturb him at first. He had dropped the simple wooden latch as he came in and his first warning of the intruder was when the latch was raised from the outside, a thin dagger sliding furtively through a crack to lift it.

A pale November moon had risen since he had retired and shone now through the open door, and in a moment, Martin half recognized the man, despite his unshaven, haggard, drink ravaged face. He raised himself on one elbow, and searched his memory for a name. It came to him quickly, one of the men who had spoken bitterly against Allard when Celeste first fastened her affections onto Sir Allard...Rafe, he thought.

"Rafe? Why are you here?"

"Yes, you crippled bastard. I'm Rafe alright. Time I reckoned with you..."

Martin struggled to prop himself up, reaching for his crutches, but Rafe forstalled him and knocked them out of his reach.

"So – how was I to know that you would fulfil a squire's duty?" he sneered, looking down on Martin, his swarthy face unkempt, his breath reeking of ale. He swayed a little as he braced himself more easily in the half dark of the barn, fingering his knife lovingly.

Martin tried feverishly to remember what he knew of this man. He had been on the edge of the group of men Sir Allard had led, handsome but lazy, sullen and whining frequently about Sir Allard's association with Celeste. At one point Martin seemed to recall that there had been some sort of half hearted challenge to Allard, which had been laughingly dismissed, and the man had slunk away, glowering angrily.

"Deserted, didn't he - the fine son in law of a knight... too high and mighty to share the prize with his men. Who did he think he was? Celeste was willing to be shared around before the mighty Sir Allard took her."

His breath came unevenly as he shoved his face nearer to Martin. His words were slurred. The smell of stale ale and sweat made Martin recoil from this crazed intruder.

"I left to follow them. Yes, I deserted, too – to follow them. You were near to death. I never expected to see you again, God rot you. You ruined my plan by being here. You'll pay for that." His face twisted in a grimace of pain. His once handsome looks were now destroyed by drink, beggary and a lust for revenge.

"I could have won Celeste for myself if he hadn't showered her with fancy promises."

His fury at the destruction of his plans was driving him beyond madness.

"All I wanted was Celeste.......I knew she would take him to Paris before anywhere else... Paris was what she knew, but The Circle followed her."

"What do you mean, followed her?"

Keep him talking, Martin thought, desparately looking round the darkened barn for a weapon with which to defend himself. He was hampered by his eye..... to see all round meant he had to turn his head in every direction but even so, he could see nothing in the darkness which would help him.

"What do you know about the Circle?" Martin asked him, staring up into the face of one who had been a comrade of sorts, at one time.

"I belonged to the Circle, stupid," Rafe snarled, "Much good did it do me. I thought the bitch would be loyal to one who was of the Circle. I was on their side. Information buys coin, and there was precious little of that from soldiering."

"You...you belonged to the Circle?" Martin was aghast, shocked at his blatant admission of treachery. He had heard about the activities of the Circle from Matthias and William on their return from Calais, and had privately wondered where the girls came from and how they gained access to the camp so easily.

"How do you think the girls knew how to get to us? How do you think they knew who was worth cultivating? I was paid well."

"You betrayed us!" Martin accused, shocked. "You would have given them details of strategies as soon as we knew where we were going."

"Very clever you are, Martin....fancy working that out so quickly!"

Rafe's knife moved nearer to Martin's sound leg, a sly expression of intent crossing his features.

"Lost one leg...Lets make it equal. That would be quite amusing."

"Rafe, why attack me? I wasn't party to Celeste in any way." Martin hoped the fear in his voice didn't betray him. The dryness in his throat made him sound hoarse.

"Allard thought he was the cock of the hoop....took Celeste.... I need to make things right for myself." Rafe's drunken babblings were just coherent enough for Martin to follow them.

"The Circle don't like deserters....they think they will cause trouble for them, so I need money to put The Circle behind me, because I'm a deserter now, see. The Circle take no prisoners....You can't have been blind to the fact that we hadn't been paid for months...That fat Coroner has money...Allard used to boast about his precious father in law and his whey faced wife...."

Rafe's face darkened as he recalled the bloated body found in the weeds at the edge of the river, just unwanted goods now to the Circle. It had been easy to take the ring for her fingers were nibbled by fishes despite the bloating of her body. Her golden hair was matted and tangled, caught in the weeds, her expressive face unrecognizable but he had stayed by her, weeping in anger, grief and frustration at how his life had become, and how hers had been snuffed out. He had taken the ring just for remembrance to start with and then its usefulness as a bargaining tool became clear to his deranged senses.

So blind rage had overtaken him, and he had vowed to seek out the family of Allard and make them pay for Allard's theft of the woman he'd become so infatuated with. At first there was no plan...he had stolen a horse and made for Calais, taking ship with what little money he had. In Sandwich, Kent, where the cog had been bound, he had met a woman who looked very like Celeste...she had golden hair and a milk white complexion....the same saucy blue eyes, but a certain coarseness in her manner quite unlike Celeste. Nevertheless, she roused the passion in him, and after some weeks he devised a plan. She was as greedy for both money and coupling as he was so when he suggested travelling West to seek the family of someone he described as a friend who might be persuaded to give them money, she was more than willing to enter into the scheming.

Martin listened to all this in silence, imagination filling details into the parts Rafe glossed over...how he had killed several times to escape the Circle as he traced Allard and Celeste, how he had stolen money to fund his passage to England...how he had lied to the girl about his true mission...his self centred lust and greed ignoring the despair of Allard's true wife.

It seemed as though the man had a need to tell his story before his punishment of Martin could be carried out...punishment for recognizing that the girl was certainly not Celeste, and that all his careful planning had come to naught.

What Rafe had not known was that the woman had a child, and although she was only kind to her daughter when it suited her, she would not travel without her. So Ennis came too. Whilst the woman fulfilled his every need, Ennis was safe, and he kept his rage under control.

Martin noticed that not once had Rafe given the woman a name. She was just the woman, or the girl. He presumed that to give her a name would somehow sur-plant Celeste in his mind, and there was no doubt that this crazed and revengeful soldier believed he had truly loved Celeste, although Martin doubted whether she had ever really reciprocated the feeling. To her he must have been just another conquest, and not really one worth bothering with.

He wondered in despair whether anyone in the house would hear him if he shouted. He thought not.

In Sherborne, matters had gone badly wrong, filling Rafe with the hot, blind rage once more. Allard had spoken hardly at all about his father and his own home, but he had often spoken of his wife's home and family, so Rafe decided to start there, where he could discover more details about Allard's father. The woman had played her part willingly enough, but was afraid to return the second time when she realised that the 'friend' was the County Coroner. Her fears were realised when Martin had appeared, and had denounced her. She had done her best, but she refused to return again which had angered him beyond belief. Fury had inflamed his lust, and she had fled from him, terrified for her life, screaming for the child to follow, but he had caught Ennis and given her a sound thrashing with his belt before passing out.

So the child had escaped a rape, at least, thought Martin.

The next part of his story was very blurred. Martin thought he was becoming tired, maudlin, and probably readying himself to make his move. It would seem that Rafe used the town unrest which brought many people out on the streets, to steal money and to search for the woman. He was hampered by the child, so he took a room in a hostelry and locked her in while searching. He was afraid the woman would return to the Coroner and tell the whole story.

He finally found her, hiding amongst the rubble in the Abbey, where his anger erupted. Martin deduced, although Rafe did not say directly, that he had beaten her senseless, and had intended to return later to take her back to the hostelry.

"The fire at the Abbey did my work for me." Rafe laughed, a harsh, cruel sound, verging on madness. "Now I just have the child to find and dispose of...and you...the loyal squire. Then I am free to deal with Allard's family members."

Martin felt under the straw mattress for his knife. He had been whittling wood so it was not a killing knife, but it was better than no weapon at all, for it was obvious that Rafe meant him serious, even fatal harm.

He realised that Rafe had no idea that Ennis was in the house. He was still looking for her. A thin idea came to him.

"Suppose I were to tell you where you can find the child," he said.

Rafe lowered his dagger arm, which had been poised to make the first cut.

"You have no idea where she is," he slurred, "let's just get this over. I'll try an amputation first, - should be fun and then we'll finish it with a killing....that appeals to my sense of justice."

"Aye, but not to mine!" Martin shouted. He kept his voice raised as loudly as possible. "The child is in the house! You will find her in the kitchen! Look for the child in the house!"

Rafe was suddenly confused. He turned towards the door as if to enter the house and check this new turn which caused him to delay for a few seconds, and also unbalanced him, but then decided against it and made a lunge for Martin's good leg, slicing deeply into it.

Martin screamed in pain...a long, anguished scream. Rafe's movement unbalanced him further in his drunken state. He staggered a little, trying to gather momentum for the next deep cut. In the darkness he stumbled against the crutch he had pulled away from Martin and fell on top of him.

"Damn you...damn you......" Rafe slashed again viciously, catching the mattress rather than Martin. He could feel the hot blood from his first deep slash pouring from Martin's leg.

Martin screamed again, loudly, "Matthias! Davy! Au secour!"

Rafe slashed again and again. Martin rolled off his mattress onto the earthen floor, trying to crawl away from Rafe's reach. He was bleeding heavily and felt sick and dizzy. He knew he could do little more to escape the crazed death blows.

Dimly he heard the shouts coming from the house, heard footsteps pounding towards the open door of the barn and in the dim light, saw Rafe's upraised dagger arm, his face contorted with hatred, lips drawn back in a snarl of fury as he brought the arm down towards Martin with ferocious force.

Chapter 13

"Whether Martin dies or not, you will surely hang." Matthias told Rafe. He was securely bound hand and foot, shaking with impotent rage. Elizabeth was binding Martin's wounds as tightly as she could, blood soaking through. Matthias had sent Davy for the local barber-surgeon as fast as possible. He prayed he would come out at night, for it was still dark and cold.

Davy and Matthias had both been roused by Martin's cries. Indeed, Matthias had been half awake for a while as he thought he could hear voices in the barn, so Martin's screams fully roused him.

They were still in the barn at present as Martin was far too badly wounded to move, and Davy and Matthias had found cords in the barn which were used to bind Rafe.

Matthias kicked him to the ground where he lay, spitting and sullen.

He was surprised that he had been able to overpower the man, so filled with hate and revenge was he, but Rafe had been drinking more heavily than he realised, he had dropped his knife in the confusion of the moment and his strength was nearly spent.

Martin was barely conscious, and the cloths Elizabeth was using became soaked very quickly. She returned to the house to find more.

It seemed an age before Davy returned with the barber-surgeon and as soon as he dismounted, Matthias sent Davy off again through the dark to rouse Sir Tobias.

Matthias knew the barber-surgeon, one Master Jacobson. Some said he was a convert from the Jewish faith and refused to use him, but Matthias had no such fears. If he could help Martin, he would do so.

It was essential to watch the man Rafe, who seemed resigned now to his capture, but Matthias was taking no chances. He stood over him until Sir Tobias arrived, with William following and Davy some way behind, worn out with the unaccustomed riding.

Elizabeth, meanwhile, was fully occupied with assisting Master Jacobson. He needed candles, hot wine or brandy and a clean place for Martin to lie. Martin moaned slightly when they moved him onto a clean mattress brought from the house. William stayed with Elizabeth, being experienced in war wounds, and helped her to dribble brandy into Martin's mouth before the wound could be stitched. Master Jacobson held his fine needle up to the candle the easier to thread. He studied Martin intently before he indicated that William should hold him steady. Elizabeth cradled his head while William steadied the leg, which Rafe would have cut away if he had been able, holding the candle as steady as he could with his free hand.

Despite the brandy and his semi-conscious state, Martin could not help but cry out as the needle pulled together the edges of the deep slash Rafe had given him. Master Jacobson's stitching was not perfect, but it drew together the flaps of skin to give the wound as great a chance as possible of stopping the bleeding. There were other cuts, but none so grave as this first one. Rafe had sliced nearly to the bone. After cleaning the other wounds with some more warm wine, Master Jacobson declared them shallow enough to be bound lightly, first asking for the white of an egg to smear over his work to assist in the prevention of infection and to seal his stitching; however, the deep stitched gash must be padded thickly and bound firmly.

Matthias was impressed with the knowledge and skill Master Jacobson showed. He guessed he had received some experience in his former life under a professional physician but was unable to use it fully because of the nature of his religion. Prejudice was a poor judge of expertise.

Martin had lost a great deal of blood and this was of some great concern. Master Jacobson recommended that Elizabeth go on the morrow to the apothecary to purchase healing herbs to poultice the wound and assist recovery - if indeed there was to be a recovery. He recommended mandragora to dull the pain and induce sleep, and yarrow infusions to fight infection. He agreed to return and Matthias negotiated a price with him for his services. He looked very grave as he left; Martin was hanging between life and death once more.

Elizabeth remained with him for the rest of the night.

At daybreak Sir Tobias and William mounted, and with the man Rafe still bound, began the journey into Sherborne, where they would take Rafe to the Castle dungeons, pending the next Sheriff's court. He refused to say a word to the Coroner, and at walking pace, with Rafe between them, the journey was tediously long. If Martin survived, they would hear the whole story, or so Rafe informed them insolently. If he died, they would not. He refused to say more, and Sir Tobias hoped the castle retainers would threaten torture to loosen his tongue.

Matthias felt drained and exhausted the next day. He was pleased that his pupils were, on the whole, receptive and obedient. He was so relieved that he had heard the noise in the barn, for if he had not, Martin would surely be dead.

Lady Alice appeared during the afternoon, anxious to help in whatever way she could. Davy had spent the morning watching over Martin, and Elizabeth had visited the apothecary to obtain the items Master Jacobson had recommended. Anthony Sewell, the apothecary, was most insistent on adding other ingredients such as valerian in a carefully measured amount as he pounded the potions and gave advice on how much to administer, and at what frequency. Lady Alice took over the task in the barn, happy to be of use, for she had enjoyed working with Martin, and was beginning to understand his loyalty in bringing her news of Allard, however distressing it had been. Elizabeth took some rest and then walked up to the village to see the apothecary again for more advice. She took Ennis with her and described carefully to Ennis how Martin had been hurt, the man being taken now to the Castle to await the next Sheriff's Court.

On the way back, they called briefly at Lydia's cottage. Whilst Ennis played with the baby, Elizabeth told Lydia of the severity of Martin's injuries. If they could avoid infection, he might live, but he had lost a great deal of blood. He was already weakened by his amputation, for although that had healed remarkably well it had still left him vulnerable.

"Martin has been very kind to me," Lydia admitted, "How can I help him?"

"You could help by keeping Ennis here with you," Elizabeth suggested.

"The child is distressed by what she has seen and experienced, and we have not yet told her that her mother has died. She is playing well with your little Freya....will you ask her if she would like to stay until I fetch her later?"

Ennis seemed pleased with the suggestion, and as Elizabeth walked home to Barton Holding, she thought Lydia was beginning to recover her sense of worth after Ben's murderous death.

There was a sense of urgency at Barton Holding as she arrived home. Davy was saddled and ready to ride for Master Jacobson for Martin was delirious and his tossing had opened his fragile wound. He had not regained consciousness since the previous evening, and Matthias was much afraid he was declining by the hour.

Matthias and Lady Alice knelt by the mattress and tried to still the restless nature of his delirium. Martin muttered and cried out, sweat pouring from him. Lady Alice bathed him constantly with a cloth soaked in scented lavender water as Matthias tried to gently hold his thrashing body to prevent any further opening of his stitches.

Master Jacobson reached them in the middle of the afternoon. His glance at Martin did not fill Matthias with hope, however, he stripped off his fine cotte-hardie and rolled up his sleeves, pinning a cloth around himself to protect his woollen tunic before baring Martin's thigh to examine the exposed wound.

"I will need assistance to hold him and to dose him with more mandragora. Do you have more strong wine?"

Lady Alice left without a word to seek what was needed. She returned with the items required, and with a candle, for, although it was still daylight, the barn was dark. She had borrowed a rough cloth from Elizabeth which she had tied around herself to protect her gown.

"No, Lady Alice," Matthias began, "This is not for you. Let me fetch Davy."

"Matthias, I can do this," she said quietly. "Just tell me what to do."

"There is little time to argue," Master Jacobson said, brusquely. "I need to still him with a dose, and he must be held immovable for the re-stitching. It matters not who does it. Dribble the wine first into him...then the mandragora dose."

Matthias held Martin's sweat soaked head between his two hands, whilst Alice tried her best to wet his lips with wine, and then the dose which Master Jacobson had measured carefully. It was not easy to do, but as it took effect, Martin's body began to relax and his fevered cries subsided into meaningless mutterings and finally fell silent.

In that moment, Matthias was afraid Martin had died, but his breathing, although shallow, did give a spasmodic rise and fall to his thin chest.

Master Jacobson went to work on the re-opened wound, using a clean wine soaked pad again to attempt to prevent infection as he carefully stitched once more. This time he was able to be more neat and precise because he had more light, with Lady Alice holding the lit the candle once her hands were free from administering wine to Martin.

"The dose I have given him is very strong," Master Jacobson told Matthias as he rolled down his sleeves.

"He should sleep through the night. As soon as he wakes, give him some more. I will leave the exact dose. He must not be left. If we can keep him still and calm, there is a chance that he may live. It depends on how successful we have been in preventing infection. It is infection in such cases that kills. He lost a great deal of blood, and I can see he is not a strong man at present."

The second use of the word 'we' warmed Matthias' heart again. He had been so much on his own in recent years. The expertise had been Master Jacobson's, but the support had been from Matthias and Lady Alice, and it pleased Matthias to hear it acknowledged.

Davy came to sit with Martin for the first part of the evening, and Matthias invited Master Jacobson into the house for refreshment before his return journey.

"I think you have more skill than the average such calling," Matthias volunteered, appraising him with an enquiring eye.

"I studied in Italy with excellent physicians, until my faith prevented further advancement," was the reply.

"We are fortunate to have your experience here then," Martin replied.

"Not everyone feels the same," Master Jacobson said, wryly. "I still have prejudice and ignorance to contend with, but that's how it has always been. When I am called to a patient, I enjoy being able to exercise my knowledge; We have converted to Christianity so my family are not persecuted here, but pockets of suspicion still remain. I will call again tomorrow if you will have me. I should like to see this young man recover. He has been through much."

"He is of the Jewish faith then?" Alice enquired after he had left.

"Originally, but, as you must be aware, Jewry was banished from our shores by Edward I and the edict has not been rescinded yet. He risks much to remain, despite his conversion to Christianity. There are a few families who have remained quietly. He is skilled beyond the calling of a barber-surgeon...and a kind man. We were very glad to find him at home. I have had some dealings with him before, but not at such close quarters as this."

Matthias found some peace in his dealings with Lady Alice, and she had acquitted herself with honour in the work she had done with Martin, both in the school-room and lately as a help-meet in the barn.

Matthias thought warmly on this after she had left with William, who rode over to escort her home.

William returned much later in the evening, willing to take a turn at watching over Martin, and Matthias was grateful for the opportunity to sleep.

Martin's condition appeared to worsen again over-night; William watched the movement of his chest to ascertain that he was still breathing. The dose given by Master Jacobson certainly gave him a deep sleep, but the pallor of his face, the sunken eyes, the unhealthy smell of his breath all gave cause for deep concern. Matthias came from his bed at midnight to allow William some time to sleep.

The morning brought its own difficulties. Martin began to rouse, but it was not a peaceful awakening. He tossed and muttered once more, tearing at the blanket covering him, and Matthias found it difficult to admin-ister the second dose which Master Jacobson had left. William had no such difficulty, however. He had seen battle, experienced treating grieviously wounded sol-diers, and with a swift movement he held the jaw open and raising Martin's head to prevent choking, poured the dose in. Martin spluttered and gagged, but eventually swallowed, and William released his head back onto the pillow.

By the afternoon, Matthias was more tired than he ever remembered feeling. He was in the schoolroom with his scholars, finding it difficult to even form his words coherently. Lady Alice and Sir Tobias arrived just as he was deciding to allow the boys some unexpected leisure, and Alice took over the schoolroom seamlessly. Matthias dropped onto his bed and fell instantly asleep.

Sir Tobias took his place by Martin. He wanted to hear the details Rafe had given Martin and he was afraid Martin would never be able to give them. He was hoping to be by Martin's side if he roused lest there was any chance of speaking, but for the present, he was content to take his turn.

Master Jacobson arrived during Sir Tobias' visit, and they spoke quietly in the shade of the barn. The barber-surgeon expressed the hope that Martin would live, for he had no apparent infection, and despite some restlessness, the stitching had held, and the changing of the dressing showed very little extra bleeding. He advised Sir Tobias to take things slowly regarding the re-telling of the story; Martin would be very weak for some time and needed to be moved to the house as soon as it was possible.

Martin woke a day later in the darkness of the barn. His good eye was but half open with drugged sleep and his limbs felt too heavy to raise a hand to rub his sweaty face. His mouth was dry, his lips felt cracked. An awareness of a firm hand restraining his leg came to him. He struggled feebly against the pressure, moaning in terror.

"Easy, Martin, easy....You are quite safe....easy now."

He recognized the voice but his brain could not drag a name to match it.

He tried to relax, hardly daring to believe the speaker. He tried to answer, but his lips would not allow him to form coherent words. He felt a brush of damp cloth wipe his lips...and again his furred tongue tried to lick his dry lips.

Sir Tobias held the soaked cloth to Martin's mouth once more. Martin sucked the moisture gladly. It was enough to re-assure him of his safety. He felt the thick padding round his injured leg with cautious hands, and relaxed into a more natural sleep.

Sir Tobias allowed his eyes to close as Martin slept

Chapter 14

Master Jacobson and Davy moved Martin carefully into the house the next week. Matthias reorganized his own sleeping chamber temporarily into the solar which he had not used since the death of his parents. Another step forward, he thought to himself, as Elizabeth fetched bedding and made up a bed for him in the spacious room. Martin protested weakly as he was carried upstairs to Matthias' sleeping chamber, but he was grateful for the change and the light of the little room enabled him to be away from the place where he had been attacked.

Davy and Elizabeth made good use of the daylight hours to scrub the floor of blood and to air the barn, disposing of the blood soaked mattress which Rafe had slashed in his drunken anger.

The child Ennis remained with Lydia for the moment. Sir Tobias would need to question her, but he was waiting for Martin to be stronger before calling on Ennis to tell her part of the story.

"Rafe will hang...there is no doubt of that," Sir Tobias told Matthias.

"We had a wasted journey to Paris," Matthias replied.

"No, far from wasted," Sir Tobias responded, soberly, "It verified the death of Sir Allard beyond doubt. For that I am grateful, Matthias. You have done my family a service. I understand now how I need to proceed with my daughter."

Matthias was silent. He hoped Lady Alice would find peace of mind and happiness in a new union. She had proved herself willing to help in all circumstances, and he had valued her help, her opinions.

He considered the child. It was pure good fortune which had led them to encounter her; he doubted whether they would have found Rafe if it hadn't been for her.

Some time later Martin was well enough to sit in the kitchen, although still very weak. The pad and binding on his leg would be in place for a while yet. He was humbled by the affection which surrounded him, and Sir Tobias, William, Matthias and Thomas the scribe were now ready to piece together the whole story.

Martin haltingly told the events as Rafe had spat them out.

It seemed to begin with an infatuation for Celeste... Martin was not sure that it was reciprocated but he had not noticed Rafe particularly to verify his claim. He was aware of Rafe only as a comrade in arms, rather a cynical, hard bitten one, not particularly astute or conscientious although he was hazy in his memories here. According to Rafe's crazed account, Rafe had been part of the Circle as an informer, and when Allard and Celeste had disappeared, he had followed, guessing their destination was Paris. It was his understanding that the Circle took no prisoners, and Celeste and then Allard were caught and killed, Celeste by drowning, Allard by stabbing. His obsession with Celeste led him to search for her body and grieve for her punishment, and then the notion of revenge swept upon him. He laid the blame on Sir Allard for the death of Celeste, and wished to wreak a suitable revenge on Sir Allard and anyone connected with him. This now became his new obsession. He had not decided how to do this until he met the girl in England who resembled Celeste in so many ways. The possession of Sir Allard's ring helped him weave his deception, together with the willingness of the girl. However, Rafe had not told the whole story to the girl – he never told Martin her name – she complicated his plans by insisting on bringing the child with her, and by suddenly losing the appetite for the plan when she realised that the so called 'friend' was none other than the Coroner. He vented his rage and frustration on the girl, who fled and hid in the Abbey. The townspeople's firing of the Abbey had completed his work for him; all he had to do now was to find the child and the squire who had unmasked the girl and then he was free to move on to Sir Allard's father, if he could discover where he was. Martin was unsure whether the Lady Alice would have been part of the plan, and he could not fill in the gaps regarding how Rafe had managed to find him.

Sir Tobias guessed it was a combination of the soldier's ability to track, coupled with local knowledge that Matthias had a guest who was an amputee...the girl would have told Rafe about Martin, and further careful local knowledge would have provided the link between Sir Tobias and the Barton household.

"My instinct tells me that Rafe killed anyone who stood in his way once he had decided on his plan of revenge," William said,

"We have no proof of that," Sir Tobias rejoined, "but by his own admission, he was a traitor. For that alone he will hang."

Matthias thought of the other unnamed girl in the ditch by the great St. Denis gate and mentally added her to the tally of Rafe's path of destruction....so many unnamed girls....at least they now had a name for Ennis.

"We thought we would never find the man we encountered in the Inn; we were wrong; it was he who found us...Martin was the lure," Matthias realised.

"Might she have been saved if the Abbey fire had not happened?" he suggested.

"I think not," the Coroner replied, "it is my belief that she had been beaten so badly that she would have died of her wounds, but we will never know...she was too badly burned. Only a segment of the ring remained to help us."

Martin had tired himself out, and as the scribe completed his writing, the meeting broke up.

"I am grateful to you, Matthias, for your unselfish help over this matter," Sir Tobias told him. "I grieve for my daughter's lost husband."

They were lingering in the yard waiting for William and Thomas to bring their horses.

"The business has been too close to me. I still find it hard to think of Allard as one who would desert. Men have their indiscretions in time of war, but to desert.... that I find hard. Lady Alice will now begin to rebuild, I hope. She has given much time to the school, which has helped her. I thank you as a friend."

Matthias laid his hand on Sir Tobias' shoulder in friendship as the Coroner mounted his horse.

William and Thomas were already mounted and they all started for home in the late afternoon, anxious now to be home before the dank November evening overtook them.

Davy and Elizabeth retired to the kitchen and Matthias pondered alone on how empty the house suddenly seemed. In the quiet he thought of Martin's fate; how could his life be improved now? Martin would certainly walk again when the wound had knitted sufficiently, and he might well be able to fashion himself a prosthetic such as they had seen on the beggar in Sherborne. It would be some time before he would be strong enough to consider what he wanted to do, whether he still wanted to leave, but he must be allowed to make his own decision. Matthias thought he would miss him.

Since he returned home he had built up a small circle of friends and acquaintances....he would like to talk more to Master Jacobson and the apothecary Anthony Sewell; Davy and Elizabeth had become very much a part of his world. William and Sir Tobias now entered into his thoughts, - he enjoyed working with them, and he had his school which did not appear to have suffered during this period of unrest. He was indeed fortunate in many ways. Lady Alice, however, he preferred not to think on. She was beyond his reach, and his dealings with her, although more cordial, could not progress beyond friendship. Sir Tobias had indicated that he knew what he must do for her, and Matthias had no doubt that an older widowed knight would be found for her in the fullness of time. His mind turned to his surprising and urgent physical need for the unnamed girl in St.Denis and wondered whether it was that which prevented him from looking on Alice with the warmth he was beginning to feel for her. He refused to allow his mind to dwell too much on that.

There was a hanging in Dorchester before Christmas. Sir Tobias and William attended to see Rafe hanged. He had killed many times, squandered his life for an infatuation and had indulged in treachery whilst serving in the King's Army. It was more than enough for conviction, and he was hanged together with others who had thieved, killed or rioted.

As they left Dorchester, they turned to see the gibbet, twisted bodies hanging as a warning to others, necks broken, limbs twirling lifelessly in the breeze. They would be left there for several days, finally removed after the crows had picked at their eyes and beggars had seized any possessions they might have left.

"I am afraid for the King," Sir Tobias murmured quietly to William. "His Grace does not govern wisely or well. It will end in noble families striving for supremacy over each other. I pray we remain safe in our quiet corner of England. It is many years since we were troubled by a visitation by his court, with all the pomp and expense that involves. Let us hope it remains that way."

William did not reply. He felt it safer to remain silent. Talk such as that could be dangerous, but he did agree with the Coroner's assessment.

Matthias had much cause to wonder, over the next few days, about the state of mind which would cause a man to hunt down the family of a person he believed to be his rival to such an extent as Rafe had done.

His own life had become a strange patchwork of late, with time spent in the schoolroom doing what he loved best, and at other times following in the footsteps of Sir Tobias, acting as his informer. He enjoyed learning, books, writing, educating; he also acknowledged to himself that he found times with Sir Tobias challenging and invigorating. Perhaps he had the best of both worlds.

The child Ennis would soon be housed with Lydia. Sir Tobias had visited her and arranged to make some repairs to her cottage if she would give Ennis a home. Lydia was willing, and the work would be done before Christmastide.

There were decisions still to be made; Martin, once recovered fully, would need help and guidance to understand that life for him would always be hard; Ennis and Lydia would need time to adjust to their new family life; Lady Alice would be forced to submit to the gentle decisions of her father, unless he was persuaded to allow her to decide on her own destiny, whatever that should be, and Matthias, for his own part, knew that he had to learn to look to the future and strive to establish his own way of family life.

Perhaps soon he would open his mother's chest and see what treasures she had stored there. Then he might begin to use the solar again, revelling in the space and light of the room where his mother and father had spent so many happy hours, but that was for tomorrow.

Author's Notes

To the best of my knowledge there was no such organization in Calais as The Circle, but soldiers certainly did desert as the wars with France began to crumble and many did return to a country where law and order was in question in many parts. They would have been penniless, starving and in some cases wounded.

The fire in Sherborne Abbey did happen in 1437, and Richard Vowell, it is believed, did shoot the fatal fire arrow, and was possibly the priest in charge of All Hallows at this time. The unrest in Sherborne is well documented, as is the attitude of Abbot Bradford. The Earl of Huntingdon's men did appear at the crucial moment and join in the riot in the Abbey for which the population were forced to pay compensation..At the same time as the unrest in the Abbey, the good people of Sherborne were collecting money for the building of the alms house and a goodly amount of money was raised, despite their having to pay compensation for the fire. The discovery of a body in the ruins is entirely imaginary. The alms house still stands near the Abbey.

Martin Cooper's injuries would not have been impossible to heal; he is a character of my imagination who was very lucky!

The young king Henry VI found decision making very difficult and relied heavily on prayer and advisors.

His greatest interest was education and learning; he was the founder of Eton College.

Richard, duke of York, mentioned as a commander at some point in France, was the father of the future Edward IV, who was one of the protagonists in the Wars of the Roses, which was the eventual culmination of the poor kingship of Henry VI.

The alms house and the need to raise compensation will be included in Matthias Barton 3.

Lightning Source UK Ltd.
Milton Keynes UK
UKHW01f2301221018
330990UK00001B/6/P